3 Bodies And A Biscotti

Leighann Dobbs

This is a work of fiction.

None of it is real. All names, places, and events are products of the author's imagination. Any resemblance to real names, places, or events are purely coincidental, and should not be construed as being real.

Table Of Contents

Chapter One

Lexy took a nibble of the pistachio biscotti. The crunch of the biscuit sounded like music to her ears. The sweet taste of the cookie combined with the contrasting creamy, soft bitterness of the dark chocolate coating created a riot of sensations in her mouth.

"Please take one, I'm trying out a new recipe and I'd love to know what you think," she mumbled around a mouthful, shoving the tray of biscotti towards the three older women.

Ruth, Helen and Nans each picked up a biscuit, and bit into it noisily. They chewed tentatively at first and Lexy felt a pang of disappointment. *Didn't they like them?*

Nans swallowed, then blotted her lips with a napkin. "It's delicious, dear." The two other women nodded in agreement.

Lexy felt her shoulders relax. Creating new recipes was a key to success for her bakery business and she loved trying them out on her grandmother, Nans, and the other ladies because they always provided an honest critique.

"Just the right scheetmess," Ruth said, slurring the last word, before reaching into her mouth and pushing down on her bottom teeth. She glanced around the table, then shrugged. "Sorry, I have new dentures and they keep slipping out."

Lexy looked around Nans's condo while she chewed her biscotti. It was a good size for an "independent living" condo in a retirement complex. Nans had moved here a year ago when she stopped driving so she could be closer to her friends and "the action". The facility provided a variety of activities and entertainment and had a decent dining room where the residents could get meals if they didn't feel like cooking.

The large complex had living quarters for senior citizens in various different situations, such as the assisted living facility and the nursing care section. Nans and the other ladies were quite independent and all had their own condos.

They were seated around Nans's dining room table, situated in between her kitchen and living room, with a view of the entire living area. The morning sun streamed in through the sliding glass door at the other end of the room. Lexy could see water dripping from the snow melting on the roof and hoped it meant winter would soon be releasing its cold grip on the area.

Lexy's eyes landed on the empty chair across from her.

"Where's Ida?" she asked, her brows wrinkling together. The four women were usually always together and Lexy found it odd that Ida wasn't there this morning.

"Oh, she'll be right along. She had an errand to run," Nans said, then looking at the plate of biscotti she added, "we'll save her a couple of biscotti. I'm sure she'll love them."

Lexy nodded and took another dainty bite. Normally she would have devoured most of the biscotti by now, but she'd noticed her jeans were fitting a little tight and figured it might be wise to cut down on the eating.

"Lets get down to business and talk about the Bertram Glumm murder," Nans said.

Lexy rolled her eyes. Nans, Ruth, Ida and Helen were amateur detectives. Though they were all well past the age of seventy, they still kept active and had been successful in solving many cases. They even had a name for themselves — The Ladies Detective Club. The problem was, they saw murder everywhere.

"You don't know he *was* murdered," Lexy said.

Nans peered at Lexy over the top of her glasses. "Of course he was dear. I think the girls know a murder when they see one."

Lexy felt a pang of guilt. Nans and the other ladies had been instrumental in helping her solve a few murders, including a couple where Lexy was the main suspect. She had just returned from a national bakery contest in Las Vegas with Nans, where she had managed to win second-prize despite having been one of the suspects in the murder of one of the judges in the contest.

The Ladies Detective Club had helped her solve the case by using old fashioned detective work and communicating on their iPads. Lexy owed it to them to at least listen.

"OK, what have you got?" Lexy grabbed another biscotti. *Had she eaten a whole one already?*

Ruth pulled out her iPad, fingers at the ready apparently, to record their conversation.

"From what I know, Bertram went into nursing care when we were in Vegas, and passed away *suspiciously* the day before we came home," Nans said.

"That's right. Bertram was only seventy-one. He was healthy as a horse. In fact, he lived just two doors down from me," Helen said, her eyes wide.

Lexy wrinkled her brow. "If he was healthy as a horse, what was he doing in the nursing care section? And why aren't the police looking into his death?"

Ruth's lips pressed together. "The police are just passing it off as another old person dying. They didn't even do an autopsy!"

"Yeah, you know how they can be," Nans said, then looking at Lexy, "not your Jack, of course. He'd listen to us...or to you." She raised her eyebrows.

Lexy felt her cheeks grow warm at the mention of Jack. She'd been dating Detective Jack Perillo for almost a year now and, while he might listen to her about other things, he had made it clear that he took a dim view of her investigating murders. She felt her stomach clench, realizing that she'd be in hot water with him if he knew what they were discussing.

"Anyway," Nans continued, "Bertram slipped on the ice and broke his leg. He lives alone and couldn't manage on his own. He was in immense pain, so they put him in the nursing section 'til he could care for himself. They had only planned to keep him there for a week."

Lexy narrowed her eyes in thought. Nans *could* be right—she usually was.

"But *why* would someone want to kill him?" Lexy asked stating the obvious question.

Before anyone could answer, the door to Nans's condo flew open and Ida tumbled inside.

"Ladies, grab your coats. There's been another murder!"

Chapter Two

The sound of chairs being scraped back filled the room as the four women scrambled to get up from the table.

"Hurry, before they clean out the room! We'll take the quick route across the courtyard." Ida motioned to them from the doorway.

"Helen, take your special glasses." Nans gestured to the table beside the door where a pair of thick, black eyeglasses sat.

"Special glasses?" Lexy echoed.

"We'll explain later when there's time," Nans said, tossing each of them their jackets from the coat rack beside the door.

They ran out behind Ida following her down the stairs to the door that led across the small courtyard, and into the nursing care section.

The nursing care section resembled a small hospital, complete with a central desk and several small rooms with hospital beds. Ida hustled down the wide hall; the women following like ducklings after a mother duck.

Ida stopped in front of one of the rooms, cast a look down the hallway and slid inside. Lexy and the others followed.

The room looked much like any other hospital room ... except for the dead body in the bed.

"It's Mavis Sanders!" Nans gasped, covering her mouth with her hands.

Lexy looked at the woman in the bed. White hair, clusters of wrinkles. She looked peaceful. *Could she have been murdered?* Lexy felt an icy finger trace its way up her spine. She quickly turned away from the bed to inspect the rest of the room.

Nothing looked out of place. Prescription bottles sat on the bedside table. The sheets were pulled up neatly. The pillows were placed under her head. It looked as if she had died peacefully in her sleep, which made Lexy wonder—just how was she murdered?

On the other side of the room, she could see Helen tilting her head at weird angles and fiddling with her glasses.

"Hurry upfff..." Ruth's dentures flew out of her mouth, clattering onto the floor and sliding under the bed.

"Crapff," she said, bending from the waist and peering under the bed.

"I'll get them." Lexy got down on her hands and knees, her butt up in the air and reached under the bed. The floor was squeaky clean. Remembering they mopped the floors in this section twice a day, she felt grateful she wouldn't get any dirt on her off-white pants.

Tilting her head sideways to get a better view, she saw the dentures had slid all the way towards the head of the bed. She scootchied further under. Feeling a little creeped out about flailing around under the bed of a dead woman, she quickly swept her hand from side to side.

Her fingers encountered something small and round. Not the dentures, but she held onto it anyway. Another long sweep and her fingers hit the dentures. Grabbing on to them, she slid her front out from under the bed. On her hands and knees like an inchworm, she was just about stand up when a grating voice rasped loudly from the doorway.

"Just what the *hell* do you think you're doing!"

Lexy swiveled her head towards the voice. Standing in the doorway was Nurse Bettina Rothschild, hands on hips, with a face puckered like she'd just devoured a sour lemon. Lexy's stomach felt like lead and her heart raced.

"We were just paying our respects," Nans said, head slightly bowed.

Rothschild's scowl deepened as she directed her glare at Lexy. "What do you have there?"

"Oh, this? Ruth's dentures slipped out. I was just retrieving them for her." Lexy held the dentures up while hiding the other object behind them in her hand.

Lexy tried to keep her hand from shaking as Rothschild took two steps towards her to get a better look.

"You're not supposed to take anything from the room. Which one of you is Ruth?" She glared at each of them in turn.

"Herethh." Ruth raised her hand, then opened her mouth to show the missing teeth. "Thsee."

Rothschild bent her large frame slightly to peer into Ruth's mouth. She looked around at the women, her eyebrows mashed together. A commotion out in the hallway stole her attention. She glanced at the door, then turned back to Lexy and Ruth.

"Fine, take the dentures and go. I don't want to see you ladies messing around in *my* hospital again!" Her rubber-soled nurse shoes let out a loud squeak as she turned and rushed off towards the hall.

Lexy handed the dentures to Ruth, then mashed her index finger into her right eye in an attempt to control her nervous eye-tic.

"You still have that eye problem?" Helen asked Lexy as they started to head towards the door.

Lexy turned to look at Helen out of her good eye and nodded.

"You know I can fix that with hypnosis."

"Yes..." Lexy's answer was cut off when she walked into Nans, who had stopped abruptly just short of the doorway.

Looking around her grandmother, she could see the exit was blocked by a steel gurney accompanied by two large men in McGreevy Funeral Home tee-shirts. Lexy recognized one of the men as Barry McGreevy, who she'd gone to high school with.

Barry squinted at her. "Lexy Baker?"

"Hi Barry." Lexy gave him a half smile. "You're taking her straight to McGreevy's?"

"Yep, natural causes. No need to bring 'em to the hospital."

Lexy exchanged glances with the other four women.

"So, you're sure she died naturally?"

"That's what the report says." Barry nodded at a clipboard hanging from the end of the gurney.

"Are you a relative?" He asked.

"No, just a friend." Lexy felt a pang at the lie and crossed her fingers behind her back.

"Oh, well I'm sorry for your loss," Barry said, then turned to the bed. "Guess I better get to work."

Lexy looked away as Barry pushed the gurney next to the bed in preparation for transferring the body onto it.

The women started to leave but their exit was blocked again, this time by Nurse Rothschild and one of the aids.

Rothschild scoured at them, then pointed at the door, "Get!"

Nans shuffled towards the door. The others fell in line. As they filed out, Lexy could hear Rothschild barking orders to the aid, her voice cold and unfeeling.

"Make sure you flush any medications labelled for this patient. And get the sheets and pillowcases to laundry right away ... we need to get this room ready for the next one A.S.A.P!"

Chapter Three

"I don't know about you guys, but that nurse scared the bejesus out of me!" Lexy said, perching on the arm of Nans's overstuffed sofa facing the other ladies in the dining room.

Ida rolled her eyes. "She's not known for her bedside manner."

"Kind of strange, a nurse being so cold and mean. You'd think she would have picked a different profession."

Helen held up the eyeglasses she'd been wearing. "Lets get these pictures uploaded."

"Pictures? What's with those glasses, anyway?" Lexy asked remembering how Nans had instructed Helen to make sure she brought them to the room.

"These are spy camera glasses!" Nans said proudly. "They can take pictures or video and no one would even know."

"We bought them on the Internet." Ruth added.

Lexy raised her eyebrows and watched while Nans took them over to her computer desk, then opened a tiny door on the arm of the glasses. She sat down at the desk. Fishing in a drawer, she produced a USB cable which she connected from the glasses to the computer.

The women clustered around the computer desk as the pictures uploaded automatically, creating a gallery on the screen.

"Does anyone see anything out of place?" Nans asked.

Lexy studied the pictures, tilting her head at different angles. Nothing stuck out to her as out of the ordinary.

"No."

"Nope."

"Not me."

"Let's watch the video."

The very bottom of the screen showed a video file. Nans double-clicked on it. A large video filled the screen. Everyone laughed as Ruth's dentures shot out onto the floor. The video zoomed in on Lexy's butt sticking out from under the bed as she fished to retrieve the dentures and they laughed even harder, causing Lexy's cheeks to burn.

"If you guys are done laughing at me now, I did find something interesting under the bed."

Four gray heads turned to look at her with four sets of eyebrows raised up to their hairlines.

She pulled the object she'd found under the bed out of her pocket and held it up.

Ida squinted at it. "What is that?"

"It's a black pearl stud earring. I found it under the bed when I was looking for the dentures."

"That could be from anyone, though," Ruth chimed in.

"True, but when I was on the floor, I noticed how clean it was. They mop those floors twice a day, don't they?"

The ladies nodded.

"So the earring must have fallen sometime between the last mopping and when we got there."

"Which means, it's highly likely the earring belongs to the murderer!" Helen said.

"Or it could have just fallen off someone's ear. It's not a definitive clue," Nans lectured.

"Did anyone notice if Nurse Rothschild was missing an earring?" Lexy joked, "She seems like a likely murderer to me."

The other women laughed, but Lexy was half serious.

"We don't even know that Mavis *was* murdered. Barry said she died from natural causes. She did look pretty old," Lexy said.

"Mavis? She was fit as a fiddle. Why, just last month we went on a golfing trip to Florida and she out-golfed everyone there. Even people in their sixties!" Ruth pointed out.

Lexy chewed on the inside of her bottom lip. It did seem coincidental that two reportedly healthy people had died in the past week.

"Does anyone know why she was there?"

Ruth tapped her lip thoughtfully. "When we were on the golfing trip she was complaining about elbow trouble. Kind of like tennis elbow, but from golfing, I guess. I think she mentioned she might be going in for an operation. She could have been there just to recover, like Bertram was. She also lived alone and probably couldn't manage by herself until she was steady on her feet."

Nans turned back to study the pictures on the computer screen. "You know, these pillows under her head look a little strange. Staged, almost. I bet the killer suffocated her with the pillows."

Ida and Ruth gasped.

"With no autopsy, we'll never know. But the nurses and doctors there must have thought she died from natural causes or they would have sent the body to the coroner instead of straight to the funeral home," Lexy said.

Nans narrowed her eyes. "They might have just assumed it was natural causes ... or they might be trying to cover something up."

"Do you think the police will believe us now?" Ruth asked.

"I don't know. Jack didn't seem to think there was any foul play in Bertram's death, but I can talk to him tonight. Maybe in light of this new death, he'll start to take notice," Lexy said.

"Great. I know you have certain persuasive powers with him." Nans winked at Lexy, causing the other women to laugh. Lexy felt her cheeks grow warm again.

"If we could only figure out *why* someone killed them, we'd have a much better chance of convincing him."

Nans pressed her lips together in a thin line. "That's true. We need to find the motive." She spun around to face the other women. "Girls, I fear we may all be in danger. The killer has struck twice this week already. If the police aren't interested in helping us, we'll just have to speed up our efforts to figure out who it is --before they have a chance to kill again."

Chapter Four

Lexy opened the back door to *The Cup and Cake*. Taking a deep breath she let the intoxicating aroma of sugar and butter permeate her senses. She never tired of that smell. Nor did she ever tire of being there. It had been her lifelong dream to open a bakery and she'd been able to fulfill that over a year ago.

"Is that you Lex?"

Cassie's voice rang out from the kitchen. Lexy poked her head in. Cassie, Lexy's assistant and best friend, was rolling out pie dough, her face flushed. Flour dotted her apron and black jeans. Her pink-tipped spiked hair bobbed up and down like a bird as she worked the dough.

"Hi."

"Hey, how did they like the recipe?"

"What? Oh, the biscotti recipe. They loved it." Lexy had almost forgotten the reason she had gone to Nans's that morning.

Cassie beamed a smile at her. Which was unusual considering she didn't smile often. Lexy noticed Cassie was really working the dough, making exaggerated movements with her hands. What was up with that?

Ignoring Cassie's odd behavior, she blurted out, "Something else happened while I was there."

Cassie looked up from her dough rolling, eyebrows raised.

"There was another murder."

Cassie gasped. "What?"

"Yep, another seemingly healthy person turned up dead in the nursing care section. Ruth assured me that this person wasn't sick. I think it's rather suspicious considering Bertram Glumm died there just a few days ago."

Cassie set down the rolling pin. "That does *seem* suspicious, but you know these people are pretty old. Maybe it's just a coincidence."

Lexy pursed her lips into a thin line. "Maybe, but Nans and the girls sure don't think so."

"And you're going to help them investigate?" Cassie asked, her thumb on her chin.

Before Lexy could answer, she was blinded by a sharp glare of light. The glare was coming from Cassies's finger, where a huge diamond ring glowed like it was plugged into an electrical outlet. Lexy felt her eyes grow wide. Her mouth fell open as she stared at Cassie.

"You're engaged!" Lexy pointed at the ring.

Cassie giggled and held her hand out to show it off. "I was wondering when you were going to notice."

Lexy felt her heart grow warm for her friend and she rushed over, smothering her in a hug. "Congratulations!"

"Thanks." Lexy saw Cassie's cheeks turn a faint shade of pink.

"Let me see." Lexy grabbed Cassie's hand, bringing the ring up towards her face. It must have been close to two carats, boasting a big round clear diamond center stone surrounded by a frame of black diamonds. "It's gorgeous. The black diamonds are perfect for you." Cassie's tastes tended to be on the Gothic side.

"John picked it out himself."

Lexy smiled thinking of John Darling, Cassie's boyfriend—fiancee now—picking out a ring. The long-haired detective was Jack's partner and didn't seem to be very sentimental, yet he'd done a fine job picking a ring that suited Cassie perfectly.

"Wow, you guys have only been dating a few months, haven't you?" Lexy switched her attention from the ring to Cassie's face.

"Six months, but when you find *the one,* you know it."

Lexy thought about her own relationship with Jack. They'd been dating for close to a year. She glanced down at her naked ring finger. Maybe Jack didn't think she was *the one.*

"I was hoping you'd be my maid of honor." Cassie startled Lexy out of her thoughts.

"Of course. I'd be honored," Lexy said.

"Great. We're not going to have anything traditional. And, of course you'll make the cake?"

Lexy nodded. "Of course."

"Perfect. Now tell me about these supposed murders."

Lexy took a deep breath. "Well, I don't know very much about them. Both victims were in the nursing care facility, but neither of them had serious illnesses. They'd both recently had an operation and were recovering there until they could manage on their own. From what Nans and the ladies say, they should have had a full recovery, but instead, they ended up dead."

"Does Nans have any idea why someone would want to kill these people?"

"That's the strange part. There doesn't seem to be any connection between the two. They have no idea what the motive could be."

Cassie narrowed her eyes. "Maybe it's some sort of deranged serial killer that picks elderly people because he knows the police will just brush it off as being a natural death."

"That's a little far fetched, isn't it? I mean if it was, he could target anyone in the retirement community, not just the people in the nursing center." Lexy felt a chill walk up her spine thinking that Nans could be in danger.

"Maybe. But I've heard of it happening before." Cassie snapped her fingers. "Or a mercy killing. Didn't you ever hear of those nurses that go around killing sick people to stop their suffering?"

Lexy thought of Nurse Rothschild. She didn't seem like the merciful type. A serial killer, maybe, but not a mercy killer.

"I don't know, I thought that stuff only happened on TV. Plus, neither one of the victims was suffering. Either way, Nans is determined to get to the bottom of it, especially since the police seem to think both deaths were natural."

"Well, what do *you* think?"

"I'm not sure whether the deaths were natural or not at this point. But I *am* sure that Jack's not going to be too happy if I start helping Nans investigate another murder."

"Yeah, that could be a problem," Cassie said. "How have things been between you two since we got back from Vegas."

Lexy felt her cheeks grow warm. Things had been good. Very good. Jack had spent the last three nights at her house, even though he lived in the house right behind hers. It had felt good to wake up next to him every day...but did she want to wake up next to him on a permanent basis for the rest of her life?

"Things have been really good."

Cassie wiggled her eyebrows. "Well, maybe you don't want to rock the boat and get him all pissed off then."

Lexy watched the light glint off of Cassie's ring. Not if I want one of those, she thought. But if Nans needed her help, she'd help her no matter how mad Jack got—even if it meant risking never getting a ring she wasn't even sure she wanted in the first place.

Chapter Five

Lexy wedged herself through the front door and prepared for the barrage of white fur and paws that usually greeted her. Sprinkles, her little Shih Tzu-Poodle mix came running from the kitchen, jumping on her and pawing at her legs. Lexy bent down and scooped her up, her heart warming at the greeting.

She dropped her purse on the couch, then released the dog, who immediately raced back towards the kitchen.

"I bet you're hungry." Lexy followed the dog, but instead of standing near her food bowl, Sprinkles was pawing at the back door.

"Oh, you want to go see Jack. I think he spoiled you when I was gone." Lexy glanced out her kitchen window to see if Jack was home. She mused about how convenient it was to have her boyfriend live in the house right behind hers ... well, most of the time.

When she'd gone to Las Vegas to compete in a bakery contest the previous week, Jack had watched Sprinkles for her. In the four days since she'd been home, the dog had wanted to go over to his house every night.

"Well, I suppose Jack won't mind if we pop over. Maybe we'll stay at *his* house tonight." Lexy opened her back door, feeling the tingle of excitement she always felt when she knew she was going to see Jack. Pulling her jacket tight around her, she picked her way through the few leftover snow mounds in the backyard with Sprinkles in tow.

Peering through the window of Jack's kitchen door, she tapped on the glass. She saw him peek out from the living room. The smile on his handsome face when he recognized her made her stomach do cartwheels. His long legs crossed the room in three strides, and he opened the door for her.

"Hi," He said, enveloping her in a hug, then brushing his lips teasingly against hers. She was about to pull him in closer when Sprinkles interrupted with a bark.

"Hi Sprinkles." Jack bent down to pet the small dog who wagged her whole body in response. "What brings you guys over here?"

"Sprinkles was scratching at the back door, so I figured we could hang out over here tonight instead of my place." Lexy started toward the living room, but Jack caught her by the waist pulling her to him and distracting her with another kiss.

"Want some tea?" He dragged her over to the table. *Did he glance nervously into the living room or was it her imagination?*

"Sure." Lexy peered around his shoulder into the living room.

Jack pushed her down into one of the chairs and started making tea. Sprinkles stood about a foot away from him waiting to spring on any errant crumbs that might fall on the floor.

"I brought Nans some biscotti today from my new recipe ... and I found out something disturbing."

Jack turned to look at her, one eyebrow raised. "What?"

"Another seemingly healthy person has died over there." Her stomach lurched when Jack made a face.

"Lexy, you're not going to start in on this murder stuff again, are you?"

"Nans and the ladies seem to think the deaths are very suspicious."

Jack came over to the table, setting one mug in front of her and taking the opposite seat. He put his mug on the table in front of him and settled his hand on top of hers.

"Honey, the people over there are old. It makes sense that there would be a high ratio of deaths."

Lexy felt her back stiffen. She hated it when Jack patronized her, but she realized she needed to keep her cool if she wanted to convince him the deaths were not natural.

"I know, but Nans seems adamant that something funny is going on. They didn't even do an autopsy on either of the people who died, so how can you say for sure?"

"Well, I assume the staff over there is competent enough to know when a death is natural or not. After all, murders are usually a bit messy."

"But, what if the murderer was very clever and made things *look* like they were natural?"

Jack chuckled. "Now you're getting overly dramatic. Why would someone go to all that trouble?"

Lexy furrowed her brow. That was the problem, she couldn't figure out why. "I'm not sure, but I think you should look into it."

Jack let out a sigh. "I'm sorry, but I'm flat out busy at work right now. In fact, I have to go back in about an hour. But I'll tell you what, if another supposedly healthy person dies over there, I'll see what I can do."

Lexy felt her heart sink—it was clear Jack didn't believe her and was just trying to placate her.

Jack started rubbing the top of her hand with his thumb which made her feel tingles in all the right places. She started to forget all about the murders. Peering into his honey-brown eyes over the rim of her mug, she thought about luring him upstairs. *He did say he had about an hour.*

The klaxon of Jack's cell phone broke the spell and he removed his hand from hers to pull it from his pocket.

"Perillo." Lexy heard him bark into the phone. She tuned out the subsequent "uh-huh's" and "yep's".

Cutting her eyes towards the living room, she got up out of the chair and started in that direction. Just before she reached the threshold, Jack caught her hand and reeled her back in.

"That was work, I gotta go." He planted a kiss on her lips and propelled her towards the back door.

"Sorry," he said. "Maybe I can make it up to you with dinner tomorrow?"

"OK," she replied uncertainly.

"Great," he said, then turned her by the shoulders to face him. "I know how much you love Nans and like to help the ladies investigate, but I'm asking you not to get involved in it. Just in case there is something going on, I don't want you to get hurt."

Lexy's eyes narrowed and she felt her face getting warm. *Who was he to tell her what to do?* Before she could voice her feelings, he brushed his lips against her forehead, opened the door, and pushed both her and Sprinkles outside.

Lexy stood on the other side of the door fuming for a few seconds before she followed Sprinkles back over to her own yard.

Opening her kitchen door, she glanced back at Jack's house. Her eyebrows knit together as she wondered two things--why she let him infuriate her so much, and what the heck he had in his living room that he didn't want her to see.

Chapter Six

Lexy surveyed the pastries in the bakery case. *Should she move the eclairs to the right, or put them behind the cannoli?* She tapped her fingernail on her front tooth, debating the best placement. Lexy was particular about how the pastries were displayed. She felt that her attention to detail is one of the things that made *The Cup and Cake* so successful.

"We're almost out of K-cups." Haley's voice broke into her thoughts from the other side of the room where she was cleaning the self-serve coffee station.

"I'll order some today," Lexy replied, her heart swelling with pride as she turned towards Haley's voice and surveyed the front area of the bakery.

She glanced through the floor-to-ceiling glass window, marveling at the beauty of the waterfall which the town was named for. Brook Ridge Falls was a quaint New England town and Lexy had been lucky to secure this space in the historic downtown section.

She had setup tables and chairs next to the window so her customers could enjoy the view while they sipped their coffee and ate their pastries. Haley, her part-time employee kept the place spotless.

Moving behind the pastry case, Lexy slid open the glass door and bent inside to get the eclairs. She picked up the tray, eyeing the chocolate covered pastry. *One of these would taste mighty good right now.*

Lexy's mouth started to water just thinking about how puff pastry filled with custard and topped off with a dab of chocolate would taste on her tongue. If she just took one from the plate, it wouldn't hurt the overall look of the display. She started to reach for the top eclair, then stopped. Remembering how she'd had to shoehorn herself into her jeans, she jerked her hand back with a sigh.

Lexy felt grateful when the sound of her cell phone distracted her from the pastry.

"Hello?"

"Hi dear, are you busy today?" Nans's voice sounded anxious.

"Umm...sort of. What do you need? Don't tell me there was another death." Lexy felt her heart plummet.

"No, nothing like that. We just might need your help on something to do with the case is all..." Nans let her voice drift off.

Lexy felt a spark of interest. She couldn't help it, she loved helping out with Nans's investigations, even if Jack disapproved.

"What is it?"

"We found out where Nurse Rothschild worked before she came here. We tried to look through the obituaries from there, but it didn't tell us anything meaningful. We figure we have a better chance of getting the real dirt by talking to the people that live there."

"Uh-huh. So, where do I fit in."

"We need an excuse to go there, of course. So, we figure we'd call them up and arrange a pet visit with Sprinkles. You know how the people in retirement centers love to see pets."

Lexy thought about Nans's proposal. What if Nurse Rothschild *was* some kind of weirdo killer? Maybe she left the other retirement center under suspicion. Or maybe her mode of operation was to move to a new one every year or so before too many people died and she got caught.

They wouldn't find out anything by looking at newspapers and company records. Nans was right, the only way to find out if any suspicious deaths happened when Rothschild was there was to ask the residents.

Her mind drifted back to Jack's warning and she felt her stomach tighten. He'd be mad if he found out that she'd been "investigating," but Nans needed her help. Besides, what harm could come from a simple pet visit to a retirement center?

"OK, count me in."

Chapter Seven

"The residents here aren't as sprightly as the people in *our* retirement center." Lexy heard Ida whisper into Ruth's ear as they approached the door leading into the Sunny Acres Retirement Home.

Looking through the glass doors, she could see why Ida might think that. The lobby was dotted with elderly, frail people dozing in chairs. A couple of them were lined up in the hall in their wheelchairs. They did seem "less sprightly" in contrast to the Brook Ridge Retirement Center where Nans and the ladies lived, which was always bustling with active seniors.

Lexy held the door open. Nans, Ruth, Ida and Helen proceeded past her and Sprinkles inside.

"Oh, you must be Sprinkles!" A bubbly, nurse's aid rushed over and bent down to pet the dog.

Sprinkles happily accepted the attention, wagging her tail and licking the woman's hand.

The commotion woke up the sleepers, who started to try to get out of their chairs.

Lexy realized most of them wouldn't be able to bend down to pet the small dog, so she motioned for them to stay seated and pulled Sprinkles over to the sitting area.

Introductions were made all around, and Nans and the girls started up conversations while Lexy showed off Sprinkles.

"I live over at Brook Ridge Retirement. I think one of our nurses, Nurse Rothschild, came from here, didn't she?" Ruth said to a pleasant woman who had introduced herself as Alma.

Alma made a face. "She sure did."

"What's that?" The man beside her said, loudly cupping his ear.

"Nurse Rothschild," Alma said in a loud voice, leaning towards him.

"Oh, she was mean." He nodded his head.

"You guys didn't like her? Why, what did she do?" Ruth asked.

"It's not any one thing ... she just didn't have much of a bedside manner," Alma said a bit guardedly.

"Oh, look at the cute dog!" Lexy's attention was drawn by two girls who ran squealing over to Sprinkles.

"Can we pet him?"

"Yes, and it's a her," Lexy said as she watched the girls cautiously approach the dog. Sprinkles loved kids and eagerly licked their hands and submitted to their gentle petting.

"What's your name?" Lexy asked the taller girl.

"Bethany. And this is my sister Kathryn."

"I'm Lexy, and this is Sprinkles," Lexy said, eliciting giggles from the girls when they heard the dog's name.

Ruth's rather loud voice caught the girls attention when she said, "Were there any strange deaths when she was here?"

Lexy's eyes went wide and she elbowed Ruth in the ribs, nodding her head towards the young girls.

"Oh." Ruth covered her mouth with her hand. The talk of death didn't seem to bother the girls at all.

"Nana San was mad her friend died when she shouldn't have," Bethany said with a shrug.

"Oh really? When was this?" Ruth asked.

The two girls looked at each other, their faces screwed up in concentration. After a second, Kathryn's face lit up.

"It was last Easter," she said.

"Yes, I remember it because Smiling Sam gave us Easter candy," Bethany added.

"Smiling Sam?" Nans looked down at the two girls, her eyebrows raised.

"He was the janitor here, but he left."

"Why did Nana San think her friend shouldn't have died?"

"She said Renee—that was her friend—was too healthy and strong. She broke her hip though and had to go to the hospital."

Lexy exchanged a look with the other ladies.

"Beeetthhhannyy," A voice echoed from down the hall. "Kaatthhryyyn."

"That's Nana San, we better go." The two girls turned and ran down the hall in the direction the voice had come from.

Ruth turned back to the women she had been talking to. "Did other people, who seemed otherwise healthy, die like that?"

"Well, now that you mention it, I did think it was a little strange when Harold Simms died," a woman with a mass of blueish-gray hair said.

"And Anita Fischer just a few days later," added a different woman, this one with a matching magenta polyester top and pants.

"WHAT?" shouted the man on the couch.

Everyone turned to look at him, then went back to their conversation. They were standing close together almost as if in a huddle. Their voices hushed. Sprinkles sat at Lexy's feet all but forgotten.

"Did the others die last year too?" Nans asked.

Blue hair pursed her lips in a thin line. "I think so ... no, that was this past summer ... no, I can't remember. All the days seem the same in here."

"Wait. It was right after Christmas. Not this past Christmas, the one before," Magenta suit said.

Nans sparkled with excitement. "Well, we should probably take Sprinkles into the other rooms."

Lexy figured Nans was trying to hurry things along so she could get back to her computer. She turned towards the door, nudging Sprinkles along.

"Oh, well thanks for bringing Sprinkles," Alma said, bending down to rub the dogs ears.

"You're welcome," Lexy said, then stepped out into the hall, heading in the direction the two girls had run off in. Maybe Nana San would have some useful information.

She was eager to get the rest of the visit over with as quickly as she could so they could double check the information they had just gleaned. If what they just learned was true, they may have just discovered the killer.

It was one of those rare early spring days when the temperature felt unseasonably warm for the time of year. Maybe it had just been so cold lately that fifty degrees seemed like a heat wave, but Lexy hoped spring had arrived early.

When they left Sunny Acres, the ladies had a hankering for ice cream, so Lexy took them to her favorite place, *King Kone*. They ordered black and white frappes for themselves and a small vanilla soft serve in a dish for Sprinkles.

Sitting around the weathered picnic table, they slurped their drinks. Lexy could feel the sun warming her back, which was a sharp contrast to the drink freezing her mouth. The creamy taste of vanilla with just a hint of chocolate hit the spot.

Sprinkles sat on the ground, her nose pressed to the cup, trying to lick up every last drop.

"Well, that certainly was an enlightening visit," Nans said.

"Yes, we'll have to double-check everything though," Ruth added.

"Naturally. But if it proves true, that's a good argument that Rothschild is the murderer."

Lexy scrunched her brows together. "But *why* would she do it?"

"I don't know, maybe she just likes to kill people. She seems mean enough."

"Well, you guys always taught me to look for the motive, but I guess liking to kill is motive enough." Lexy wrapped her lips around the straw and tried to pull some of the frozen frappe up through it.

"Perhapssth," Ruth said popping her dentures back in.

"There might be another motive. Or it could all be coincidence. Either way, I think we need to look a little deeper into Nurse Rothschild's past," Nans said.

Lexy nodded. "First we should verify Rothschild was even at Sunny Acres when those deaths occurred. Then we should try to determine if the deaths really were suspicious."

"That's going to be tough. Those people didn't seem to have very good memories." Ida pried the plastic lid from the top of her frappe and poured some of it into Sprinkles's cup.

Lexy watched the dog lap at it energetically, the cup inching forward with each lap. "I wish we had a way of getting them to be more sure of the dates, otherwise we may waste a lot of time."

"I know exactly how to do that," Helen said. "I can just hypnotize them."

Lexy chewed the inside of her cheek, remembering how Helen had helped her recall the details of a murder scene once by hypnotizing her.

"Would that work for this?"

"Of course, they'll be able to clearly remember the dates and circumstances."

"We'd have to be careful, I don't think Sunny Acres would be too keen on us hypnotizing their residents."

"Of course, I'll do it very subtly. Maybe we can arrange another visit with Sprinkles and you all can keep a lookout while I do the dirty work."

Lexy's brows furrowed together. *Would hypnotizing these elderly people have any adverse side effects?*

Helen looked at Lexy, and as if reading her thoughts, said, "Don't worry, dear, it's all perfectly safe ... they may even find they have a renewed sense of vigor after I'm done with them."

Lexy's eyes narrowed. "OK, well if you're sure..."

The ladies nodded, then slurped the rest of their frappes.

"Let's not forget the earring Lexy found either," Nans stood and collected the cups from everyone. "We need to try to find out who that belongs to. If it's Rothschild's, it could add to our case."

"We should also try to figure out if there is anything else going on. Like if she has any unusual financial transactions, or if something strange is happening at these facilities when the deaths happen," Ruth said.

"Did you get a chance to feel Jack out about the case?" Ida said wiggling the first two fingers of each hand in the air to resemble quotes when she said the "feel Jack out" part.

The other women snickered and Lexy rolled her eyes. "He doesn't think anything funny is going on. He said maybe if more people die, he'd look into it."

"So, he probably doesn't want you investigating it," Nans said.

Lexy's heart clenched and she looked down, picking at an errant thread on the bottom of her tee-shirt. "No."

"Well, that's okay dear, men can be a little strange at times. But I always say, *What they don't know, can't hurt them*," Nans said, turning with a wink and heading towards the car.

Chapter Eight

Lexy was still thinking of Nans's words when she met Jack for dinner. Except it was more like,what he didn't know couldn't hurt *her*. Not that she would lie to him, but who said she had to give him every little detail about her day?

Lexy looked enviously across the table at Jack's prime rib. Glancing back down at her skimpy salad, she speared a piece of lettuce with her fork and brought it to her mouth.

"Is that all you're having?" She looked up to see Jack looking at her quizzically as he buttered a piece of bread.

"Yes. This is very healthy," she said not wanting to admit that her shrinking wardrobe was the reason.

"Uh huh...," Jack said, his eyes sparkling with humor, then added. "It wouldn't be because your getting a little muffin top, would it?"

Lexy felt a jolt of panic. *Had she gained that much weight?* She looked down at her hips, feeling her face grow warm.

Jack laughed at her response. "I'm just kidding Lexy, you look fine."

Lexy shifted the topic to something other than her weight. "So, I saw Cassie's gigantic ring. I had no idea they were going to get engaged, did you?"

Jack's arm knocked over his water glass and he jumped up to blot it from the white tablecloth.

Lexy wondered if the topic of marriage made him nervous. Or maybe it was just talking about it with *her*. Maybe Jack didn't want to discuss marriage with someone who had a big muffin top.

Jack cleared his throat. "Umm ... yes, John was all nervous about asking her. He wasn't sure she'd say yes. He asked me to be the best man."

Lexy's heart gave a little thump picturing her and Jack at the alter together—even if it would be on either side of the bride and groom.

"Cassie asked me to be the maid of honor. Actually, we have a dress fitting to go to tomorrow. Seems like it is all happening so fast. I guess they plan to get married as soon as possible."

Jack nodded, pausing to chew a bite of his steak and wash it down with some wine. Lexy munched a cucumber and eyed the bread bowl.

"I just hope we can wrap this case up by then so he can focus on his honeymoon."

"Oh, what's the case you're working on?"

"It's a local drug ring."

Lexy's eyebrows shot up. "Here, in Brook Ridge Falls?"

"I know, you wouldn't think that sort of thing would happen here, but it happens everywhere. These are mostly small time, though. Dealing pot, hash and some prescription drugs that they probably steal from their parents medicine cabinets."

Lexy nodded, feeling a bit relieved that Jack wasn't going against some big drug lord with a gang of armed henchmen.

"So what did *you* do today?" Jack asked.

Lexy felt her shoulders grow tense. She figured if she told Jack the *real* reason for her visit to Sunny Acres, he'd be mad. The problem was, she wasn't a very good liar. He knew that every time she got nervous, her eye started to twitch. And she got plenty nervous when she lied to Jack.

"I took Sprinkles on a pet visit to Sunny Acres Retirement Home."

"You did? I didn't know you were interested in doing that sort of thing," Jack said, studying her carefully.

Lexy shifted uncomfortably in her chair.

"I always take her to Brook Ridge Falls Retirement Center and I figured I should spread the love around." Lexy shrugged.

Jack pushed his plate away and leaned back in his chair, narrowing his eyes at her. "Did you do this by yourself, or did someone go with you?"

Lexy felt her heart beat faster. She busied herself with looking down into her salad bowl. "Nans and the ladies came with me. You know, they hardly ever get out."

"Uh-huh."

Lexy nodded, still focused on chasing the last pieces of salad with her fork.

"Lexy, look at me."

Lexy's head started to swim. She felt the pit of her stomach drop and it wasn't because of the lack of food. Worst of all, her damn eye started twitching. She looked up at Jack, squinting her eyes in the hopes it would stop the twitch.

"This has something to do with those deaths, doesn't it?"

Her stomach clenched. "Sort of," she said in a small voice.

Jack sighed and rubbed his face with his palms. "I thought we agreed that you wouldn't investigate that."

Lexy bit her bottom lip, her eyelid jumping with every heart beat. She didn't recall actually agreeing to that. In fact, it seemed more like Jack *told* her she wouldn't investigate it, which made her kind of mad, because she didn't need *him* telling her what to do.

She sat up straighter in her chair, poking her index finger into her eye to stop it from twitching.

"I don't see what the problem is since *you* don't seem to think the deaths were suspicious in the first place."

"They probably aren't. But even so, the things you do when you investigate can be a little dangerous."

Lexy didn't bother to answer him. Instead, she pushed what was left of her salad away. Feeling a chill from the air conditioner, or possibly from

Jack, she pulled her periwinkle colored wrap tight around her shoulders.

Her heart squeezed when Jack reached across the table and grabbed her hands. His warm brown eyes drilled into hers and she felt a little uncomfortable at the emotion she saw in them.

"It's just that I love you so much, I don't want anything bad to happen to you, and you do tend to put yourself into danger when you are investigating something."

Normally his words would have melted her heart, but not tonight. She was too mad at the fact that he just assumed she would do as *he* said. Suddenly, Lexy felt glad she wasn't wearing his engagement ring.

She jerked her hands out from under his and stood up. "I think I can take care of myself," she said. "In fact, I think I'll just take myself home right now."

"Lexy wait—"

But she didn't wait to hear what he had to say. She turned on her heel and stormed out of the restaurant, ignoring the hurt look on his face. She was determined to do whatever she wanted, no matter what Jack Perillo said.

It wasn't until hours later when she was settled on her couch, with Sprinkles, eating a box of biscotti and chocolate ice cream that she realized Jack had said he loved her.

Chapter Nine

Lexy felt dizzy looking at all the wedding gowns. Silk, lace, pearls, rhinestones. How could anyone pick just one? Leafing through the rack, she tried to picture each one on Cassie.

"Do you have any idea what style you want?" She asked over her shoulder at Cassie, unable to peel her eyes away from the dresses.

"Actually, I have a few set aside I want to try on, but I'm waiting for the others to get here." Cassie turned from the rack with a beaded mermaid style dress in her hand. "This one would be perfect on you."

Lexy spun around and gasped, holding her hand out for the dress. It was a slightly off white color which created a dramatic contrast to the thousands of hand-beaded pearls and crystals.

She held it up in front of her and turned to the mirror. The strapless top tapered into a tiny waist which continued tight against the hips then flared out down around the knees. It was gorgeous. Lexy looked down nervously at her hips and tried to pull the dress flat across them. Too tight.

"I don't think I'll be needing a wedding dress anytime soon." Probably a good thing too, since she clearly needed time to lose a few pounds.

The bell over the door jangled and Cassie swiveled towards the sound. "Here they are."

Lexy turned to see two women heading in their direction.

"Lexy, these are my cousins, Justine and Sam."

Lexy shook hands with the women, her gaze lingering on the short blonde Cassie had introduced as Sam.

"You look familiar, do I know you?" Sam echoed her thoughts.

"I'm not sure. You look a little familiar too. Maybe I've seen you at my bakery, *The Cup and Cake*?"

Sam pursed her lips and narrowed her eyes. "I don't think so."

A sales clerk joined the group. "Are you girls ready?"

"Yes. I put a dress on hold out back to try on," Cassie said.

"Of course, come this way."

Cassie followed the clerk leaving Lexy, Sam and Justine to engage in small talk.

"What do you think her dress choices look like?" Justine asked.

Lexy raised her eyebrows. "It's hard to say. I've never even seen her in a dress before. I'm surprised she's wearing one for the wedding."

Sam and Justine giggled.

"I don't think she'd go for strapless. And nothing too girly." Sam looked through the dresses on the rack, then pulled one out. "Something plain like this maybe."

Justine made a face at the plain white silk sheath. "Boring."

"Maybe something simple, in an ivory color," Lexy said.

"That you can wear a black leather jacket over."

They all laughed at Sam's joke. Cassie's taste in clothing was more biker than chic. She usually wore jeans, tee-shirts and black leather. Lexy couldn't even imagine her in a white wedding dress but the thought brought a smile to her lips.

"What do you guys think?" Cassie had snuck up behind them and the three girls spun around.

Lexy felt her eyes grow wide and her mouth open in a big O. Her gasp of surprise echoed those of Sam's and Justine's.

Instead of the traditional white wedding dress they were all expecting, Cassie stood in front of them in a gorgeous deep red silk dress that flowed down to the floor, puffing out at the bottom and tapering to a long train in the back. The whole thing was accented with black-beaded decoration.

"You look stunning!"

Lexy saw Cassie's cheeks turn red. "Really?"

"Yes," All three girls said at once.

"I love it. It's so ... you."

Cassie looked at herself in the mirror, turning to check out each side. She touched the pink spiked hair on the top of her head. "I'll have to dye this red to match, but I think this is the one."

Lexy felt a rush of warmth for her friend. Judging by the smile on her face, Cassie was truly happy. She'd found the right man and the right dress. Dismissing the nagging, petty jealousy that tried to creep into her thoughts, she gave Cassie a hug.

"I'm so happy for you."

"Thanks," Cassie said, then turned to the others. "I've picked out a bridesmaid dress I want you guys to look at. If you don't like it, we can look for something else, but I think it will be perfect."

As if by magic, the clerk appeared holding a slinky black sheath. The sleeveless dress had a plunging V-neck and clung tight all the way down. Lexy eyed it dubiously, while sizing up the other two girls who were rail thin. She felt her stomach clench, wondering how her "muffin top" would look in the dress and cursed Jack for mentioning it, even if he was only joking.

"What size would you like?" Lexy started realizing the clerk was looking at her.

"Size six." Lexy could have sworn the clerk looked down at her hips and raised her eyebrow in a question, but she turned so quickly Lexy couldn't be sure.

While the clerk disappeared to find the dresses in the proper size, Lexy turned her attention back to Sam.

"It's still bugging me that I can't place where I know you from." She tapped her index finger on her front tooth.

"Oh, you probably saw her when you were visiting Nans. Sam works at the Brook Ridge Falls Retirement Center," Cassie offered.

"You do?"

Sam nodded.

"Oh, which part?"

"In the nursing care facility," she answered. Then her eyes narrowed. "Hey, was that you the other day that caused such a ruckus when Mavis died?"

Lexy felt her cheeks grow warm. "Well, umm ... now that you mention it, that was me. I wouldn't say it was a ruckus, though."

Sam raised her eyebrows. "Nurse Rothschild was fit to be tied. Who were those women you were with."

"My grandmother and her friends." Lexy debated telling Sam about their investigation, but decided it was best to keep quiet and get all the information she could out of her while she had the chance. "They knew Mavis and wanted to pay their respects."

"Really?" Sam wrinkled her brow. "How did they even know she had died?"

"Oh word gets around quick over there." Lexy shifted on her feet uncomfortably, suddenly feeling like she was being interrogated when *she* was the one that wanted to do the interrogating.

"Nurse Rothschild doesn't seem very nurturing."

Sam laughed. "Yeah, she's not known for her bedside manner."

"Seems like she would be mean to the patients … does she even like them?" Lexy probed.

Sam looked at her sideways. "I'm not sure what you're getting at."

"Well, we were just wondering, I mean with all the deaths lately..." Lexy let her voice trail off.

Sam hesitated before she answered, her brow knit together and Lexy saw a cloud pass over her face. "Well, she does seem cold and uncaring. I did hear her say something about one less old person being fine with her when Mavis died."

Lexy felt her stomach flip. *Now* she was getting somewhere. She was just about to dig a little deeper into Nurse Rothschild's personality and motive when the clerk returned with three dresses, the hangers clacking as she doled them out to each girl.

"You can change over there." She pointed towards a row of doors.

Lexy took her dress into the room. Staring at it on the hanger, she did have to admit it was stunning and would look fabulous on the right body. But, did she have the right body?

She stripped down to her bra and underwear and slid the dress off the hanger. Her fingers reveled in the soft silk material as she unzipped the back.

Slowly she slid it over her head and arms. The dress bunched around her waist and she went about straightening it out, pulling and tugging. It felt like putting on a girdle.

Her frustration growing, she pinched the material and tried to situate it around her hips so it didn't ride up. She managed to smooth it down, but it was so tight she had images of the dress ripping open if she tried to sit down. To make matters worse, she could only zip the back up halfway.

Lexy opened the door to her dressing room. Her heart plummeted when she saw Sam and Justine already in their dresses and looking stunning. She tried to push down the anger she felt. *Obviously the dresses must run small.*

She felt her cheeks flame when everyone turned to look at her standing in the open doorway holding the back of her dress together, the material around her hips and stomach so tight, it was practically bursting at the seams.

The sales clerk tilted her head to one side, raised an eyebrow and said, very loudly, "a larger size, then?"

Lexy nodded, then backed up into the room, shut the door and waited for the clerk to return.

It turned out the wait was worth it. Even though Lexy hated the thought of putting on a size eight dress, it did fit her perfectly and looked amazing. Her spirits renewed, she opened to door to show the others.

Cassie stood alone in the dress room. Her face lit up when she saw Lexy.

"It looks gorgeous on you!"

"Thanks." Lexy glanced around the room. "Where's everyone else?"

"Oh they had to get back to their jobs, but they loved the dress too … so is it a go, then?"

Lexy nodded. The dresses were beautiful and she was happy everything was going so well for Cassie, but she couldn't help but feel a bit deflated as she went back into the dressing room to change out of the dress.

An avid clothes horse, she'd looked forward to the excursion to the dress shop, but now she'd just felt depressed. Not only had she screwed up the opportunity to pump Sam for more information on Nurse Rothschild but she'd also gone up a dress size. Lexy wasn't sure which one made her feel worse.

Chapter Ten

"What the *hell* are you doing?"

Lexy stood frozen in front of the food processor, a cup of black beans in her hand. She turned to see Cassie in the doorway looking like she just drank sour milk.

"I'm making some healthy brownies."

"With beans?" Cassie cocked an eyebrow, venturing closer and peering into the food processor.

"Well, you're always saying we should start a healthier line of pastries, and, well ... I do need to start eating better."

"Does this have anything to do with having to get a larger dress size at the shop?"

Lexy felt her cheeks getting warm. "That, and Jack teased me about having a muffin top."

Cassie gasped, "He did not!"

Lexy nodded.

"Well, you don't. You look fine. What's wrong with him? Doesn't he know better than to say something like that to a woman, even if he is teasing?"

"Clearly not," Lexy said, pouring agave nectar into a measuring cup.

Cassie leaned against the counter. "So, are you mad at him."

"I guess you could say that, but not because of the muffin top remark." Lexy gestured for Cassie to pass over the cocoa powder and eggs, which she added to the food processor along with the agave.

"He told me he didn't want me to investigate the murders at Nans's place. Even though he doesn't think they *are* murders. Anyway, I don't need anyone telling me what I can and can't do." Lexy added coconut oil, vanilla extract, a pinch of salt, and instant coffee to the food processor, slammed on the lid and started it up.

"I absolutely loved your dress. And the bridesmaid dresses." Lexy changed the subject to a happier one.

Cassie beamed at her. "I'm so glad you liked it. I know its not traditional, but you know me."

Lexy laughed. "Your cousins seem nice. Isn't it funny that Sam works at the retirement center. I guess it's a small world."

"Yeah. I'm happy to see she has a good place to work and is straightening up her act. She used to be the black sheep of the family—into drugs and all kinds of bad stuff."

Lexy stopped the food processor and scraped the contents out into a pan. She took a tentative lick from the spatula, expecting it to taste like a chocolate burrito. Instead she found it was quite good.

"Hey this is pretty good. Want some?" She held the spatula out to Cassie, who took a taste.

"Surprising. You can't even taste the beans."

"We'll see how the brownies come out once they are baked. I might take them over to Sunny Acres." Lexy slid the pan into the oven.

Glancing around the kitchen, she leaned over and whispered to Cassie, "Helen is going to hypnotize some of the residents to make sure we get the dates of the suspicious deaths right, and then we can correlate them to when Rothschild worked there."

Cassie raised an eyebrow but kept silent.

Thirty-five minutes later, Lexy was staring at a warm brownie on her dish. Grabbing a fork, she cut off a corner. They were moist and rich looking. She took a sniff, breathing a sigh of relief that it didn't smell like beans. She put the fork in her mouth and was surprised at the rich chocolate taste. Not a hint of beans in there, yet the brownies were healthy, low in calories and rich in fiber. She might be onto something.

She scoffed down the brownie, then cut the rest of the pan into bite size pieces and arraigned them in a bakery box that had her logo, phone number, and address. No reason why she couldn't do a little advertising while she was passing out brownies and helping to hypnotize the residents at Sunny Acres.

"Are you guys back already?" The nurse's aide looked questioningly at Nans before bending down to pet Sprinkles.

"We promised some of the people we met the other day that we'd come back and bring some treats from my granddaughter's bakery." Nans pointed to the box Lexy was holding. "She owns *The Cup and Cake*, you know."

Lexy opened the box and the smell of chocolate wafted out, pulling the aide closer.

"These look delicious, may I?"

"Of course." Lexy handed her a napkin from the pile she had stashed in her jacket pocket.

"We're going to visit a few of our new friends in their rooms today, is it okay if we head down?" Nans jerked her head towards the corridor.

"Sure," the aide said. Then as they turned, she added, "Thanks for the brownie!"

Nans had been smart enough to get Alma's room number when they were there the other day, and she headed straight for it. This section of Sunny Acres was setup more like a nursing home and the rooms were single bedrooms, most of which stood with their doors open.

They reached Alma's room, and Helen tapped on the door to catch her attention.

"Oh hi. I didn't expect to see you people back here so soon."

"We wanted to bring you some brownies that Lexy baked today." Lexy offered the box and a napkin to Alma who choose a brownie.

Sprinkles jumped up on the chair next to Alma, and she broke off a corner of the brownie to feed to the dog. Helen sat in the chair next to Alma.

"How are you feeling today?" Helen asked.

"Okay. A little tired, but then I do most days. I don't have much ambition anymore so I mostly sit here and watch T.V."

Lexy noticed Helen take Alma's hand, holding it by the wrist. Nan's and Ruth stood back by the door eating brownies, Ruth leaned against the door jam and watched down the hall in a subtle attempt to "stand guard." Lexy stood nearby with the box of brownies in her hand. They had planned earlier that if anyone looked like they were going to come into the room, the three of them would cluster around the door and distract them by offering them a brownie.

Lexy watched in fascination as Helen talked softly to Alma, getting her to relax. The woman's eyelids fluttered and then closed.

"Alma, do you remember those suspicious deaths you were telling us about?"

"Yes."

"Can you tell me the dates."

Alma was silent for a moment, then rattled off a few dates, which Ida wrote down on a piece of paper.

"Good. Alma, I'm going to tap your knee and when I do, you'll wake up with a renewed sense of vigor and a positive attitude. You won't remember anything about this conversation, but you'll have boundless energy and a zest for life like you did in your youth."

Alma nodded. Ruth tapped her knee. Alma's eyes drifted open. She took a bite of the brownie.

"These are delicious. Thanks so much for bringing them." She finished off the brownie, crumpled up the napkin and threw it into the trashcan. "Well, it was nice visiting you ladies, but I feel a little restless. I think I'm going to go for a long walk." She bounced up from her chair like a teenager and headed for the door.

Lexy stared after her, then turned to Helen. "Wow, her attitude really changed, was it that part you added at the end?"

Helen nodded. "Just a little gift to make her days brighter. Now, shall we move on to the next person?"

Forty minutes later, they were out in the parking lot trying to squeeze themselves and Sprinkles into Lexy's VW beetle. Lexy marveled at how Helen, Ruth, and Ida could contort themselves into the tiny back seat. Ruth said their daily yoga practice helped.

Lexy started up the car and a strange smell assaulted her nostrils, causing her nose to wrinkle. "What's that smell?"

Nans blushed. "Sorry, dear ... I have gas."

"Oh, you too?" Ruth asked.

"I thought it was me," Ida chimed in. "I think Alma had it too. I heard a few duck quacks when she sprinted out of her room in front of me."

Nans glanced sideways at Lexy, who was busy fumbling with the buttons to roll down the windows. "Lexy, what was in those brownies, anyway?"

Lexy looked back at her sheepishly. "Black beans."

All four women said, "Ohh," at the same time, then Ida added, "If you'd told us, we could have dosed up on Beano."

Nans, Ruth, and Helen laughed.

Nans half-turned in her seat so she could talk to all four of them. "Even though we have to put up with some gas, I'd say the trip was a big success. Before we came, I researched the dates Nurse Rothschild worked at Sunny Acres and she did work there on the dates Alma and the others mentioned. Now we just need to find some concrete evidence so the police can arrest her before she kills someone else."

Chapter Eleven

"This looks like a high quality pearl. The setting is 18K." Nans squinted into the magnifying glass, causing her eye to look gigantic from the other side.

"I bet that's the type of earring one would wear all the time," Ruth said.

"Which means, someone must have seen her wearing it ... or, better yet, there might be pictures of her wearing it," Ida added.

Ruth grabbed her iPad and started searching. "I'll look at the photos from our website and Sunny Acres' website to start. Maybe we should look into other places she's worked too?"

"That's a good idea. We could visit them like we did Sunny Acres, and find out if there's been any deaths that seem unusual," Lexy said.

"Wait a minute." Ruth whipped off her glasses and took the magnifying glass from Nans. She bent over the iPad holding the magnifier at varying distances. "Isn't that the janitor from *our* nursing facility in this picture?"

Everyone clustered around the iPad. Lexy bent down to get a better look.

"Yes, I recognize him from when we were down there the other day," Lexy said. "And he's standing right next to Nurse Rothschild."

"That means, they know each other," Nans said, then added, "Does anyone else think it's odd that they worked at Sunny Acres together and now work here together?"

"Maybe they do the killings together?" Ruth narrowed her eyes at the picture.

"Or maybe Nurse Rothschild has some hold on him and gets him to do the killing for her," Helen said.

"*Or* maybe he's the killer and Rothschild has nothing to do with it!" Ida added.

"Maybe we should be looking into him too," Lexy said just as her cell phone notified her of a text. She rummaged in her purse and pulled it out. It was a simple two word message from Jack.

Dinner tonight?

Lexy wondered if that was his version of an apology. Should she accept? Lexy wasn't sure if she wanted to, so she stuffed the phone back into her purse, and decided to answer the text later.

"First, we should find out if either of them were even there the nights of the murders. Maybe it will rule one of them out," Nans said.

"Right. How do we do that?" Lexy asked.

"One of us could blunder down there and pretend we were lost or looking for something then try to sneak a peek at the schedule. But, the schedule probably only lists the hours for the coming week so it wouldn't tell us who was on duty when the murders happened," Ruth said. "I wonder if they have it in a database, maybe I can hack into it."

"Cassie's cousin works down there as a nurse's aid. Maybe I could ask her. I don't know if she'd remember the exact dates though."

"You mean you have an *inside* person down there, and you didn't tell us?"

Lexy felt her heart jump as all four women stared at her. She raised her hands, palms out. "Hey, I just met her this morning."

Nans looked at her watch. "Oh dear, where has the time gone? Lexy, you better get down there and see if your friend is on duty. Ruth and Helen, you keep searching for pictures. Ida, find out about this janitor character."

Nans grabbed Lexy's coat and shoved it in Lexy's hands then pushed her towards the door, turning the knob to open it for her.

"Jeez, what's the hur—"

Lexy's protest was cut off mid-sentence as the door opened to reveal Jack Perillo standing on the other side.

###

Lexy's heart jerked in her chest when she saw Jack.

"What are you doing here?" They both said at the same time.

Jack looked down at her. "You go first."

"I was just visiting Nans," Lexy said innocently.

"Me too."

Lexy narrowed her eyes. Jack and Nans were good friends, even before she met him. The house Lexy lived in now had been Nans so Jack and Nans were neighbors for many years. Nans and the Ladies Detective Club also helped Jack out on cases occasionally, but she didn't realize Jack usually just popped over to visit Nans in the middle of the day.

"Did you get my text?" Lexy's heart melted at the puppy dog look on Jack's face.

"I just got it," she said, not wanting him to think she had ignored him.

"Oh, well what about it?"

Lexy chewed her bottom lip. Maybe she had overreacted a little bit the other night. Jack was standing close to her, he looked good and she was starting to get all tingly. Having dinner with him seemed like a great idea. Not only that, but she really just wanted Jack to get out of the way so she could go talk to Sam.

"OK."

"How about steaks on the grill?" Lexy's mouth started to water. Jack cooked a mean steak.

"Sounds good. So, are you here about a new case or something?"

Jack shifted his feet and cast a glance at Nans. Lexy turned and looked between the two of them. *What was going on?*

"You could say that." She noticed the gleam in Jack's eye, which made her even more suspicious.

"Oh, well I want to hear about it."

"Sorry sweetie, this one is just for Nans." Jack stepped to the side unblocking the door. "Were you going somewhere?"

Lexy felt her stomach clench. She didn't want to tell Jack where she was going. He'd probably tell her not to get involved which would start the fight all over again. Lexy was tired of fighting.

"I was just leaving. I have a bakery to run, you know," Lexy said, feeling her eye start to twitch.

"OK, see you tonight?" Jack seemed just as anxious for her to leave as she was.

Lexy backed down the hall. "Yep, see you then." She turned and made a big show of walking towards the door to the parking lot.

As soon as she got out of sight, she backtracked toward the hallway that led to the nursing care section.

Lexy was sauntering between the rooms, trying to look like she belonged when she spied Sam inside what looked like a storage room. She tapped on the partially open door. Sam whirled around knocking over some pill bottles in the process.

"Sorry, I saw you in here and thought I'd say hi," Lexy smiled sheepishly.

"Hi, How are you?" Sam said. Lexy noticed her face was flushed and her hands fluttered nervously at her sides. *Did she startle her that much*?

"I'm great. Boy, Cassie's dress sure was a stunner, wasn't it?"

"Yeah. Did you get yours to fit?"

Lexy felt her cheeks grown warm. "Yes, it looked great ... I think those sizes run small," she added quietly.

"I was wondering something ... about the night Mavis died." Lexy felt her heart beat pick up speed, her palms got a little clammy as she glanced down the aisle to make sure no one would over hear them.

Sam straightened her spine and her eyes narrowed. "What?"

"I was wondering if you noticed whether Nurse Rothschild was working that night?"

Sam relaxed a bit and leaned back against the counter, chewing on her bottom lip. "Yes, she was. I remember because I was also working. We had a midnight to eleven shift, and that morning we discovered she had passed. Why?"

Lexy stared at Sam, and then decided to take a chance. "You don't think she could have something to do with Mavis's death, do you?"

Sam's eyes went wide. "What do you mean?"

"Mavis was very healthy, so was Bertram Glumm, yet they both died here in the past couple of weeks," Lexy whispered.

Sam's eyes darted around the room and her hands got fidgety again. "I never thought about that. It's possible, but I wouldn't know anything about it."

"Ah, well it was just a silly thought." Lexy backed out of the doorway. "I'll let you get back to work."

Sam glanced behind her. "Right. Nice to see you again."

"Same here."

Lexy backtracked into the hall and went straight to her car, peeking out the window into the parking lot first to make sure Jack wasn't out there.

She felt satisfied with the day so far. She'd discovered Nurse Rothschild was working when Mavis died and she'd be eating thick, juicy steaks with Jack for dinner. But as she drove away, a couple of things nagged at the back of her mind. Why was Sam so nervous, and what the heck were Jack and Nans up to?

Chapter Twelve

"My, that certainly is an interesting cake," Ruth said, as she eyed the triple layer dark chocolate confection Lexy balanced on the palm of her right hand while she walked it to the glass table where Ruth, Nans, Helen and Cassie were seated in the front room of her bakery.

"It's a trial run for Cassie's wedding cake." Lexy put the cake on the table and stood back admiring it. It was a triple-tier cake in miniature. The icing was almost black and as smooth as silk. Embedded around the edges of the cake were edible silver-colored studs and spikes.

Cassie sat next to Nans, grinning ear to ear. "I love it!"

"Now, let's see if it tastes as good as it looks." Lexy slid a knife into the bottom layer and sliced off five pieces. She put them on plates and handed them around the table.

"Hey, where's Ida?" Lexy said, her eyebrows wrinkling together. The ladies always went everywhere together and it was strange to see Nans, Ruth, and Helen without her.

Nans paused, her cake-laden fork halfway to her mouth. "Her boyfriend has a bad case of gout. She's back at the center watching over him. He's in terrible pain."

"Ida has a boyfriend?" Cassie's eyebrows raised up to her hairline.

Helen nodded. "Us older people have urges too, you know."

"Too much information, Helen," Lexy said, screwing up her face and pushing her cake plate away, amidst laughter from Nans, Ruth and Helen.

"The cake is delicious," Nans said, licking frosting from the tines of her fork.

Lexy beamed with pride as the others murmured their agreement.

"And the design?" She asked.

"Fits Cassie perfectly," Nans answered.

"It's exactly what I wanted." Cassie scraped the frosting from her plate with the side of her fork.

"When is the wedding, dear?" Ruth asked.

Lexy felt a pinch of envy in her gut when she saw Cassie's eyes get all dreamy at the mention of her wedding. Then she immediately felt bad because she was truly happy for her friend. Maybe the pinch was hunger pangs—she hadn't eaten much lately.

"Two weeks," Cassie answered, then turned to Lexy. "Don't forget the rehearsal is on Thursday."

Lexy nodded, then turned her attention to Nans. "Did you and Jack finish talking about your case yesterday?"

"Yep," Nans said. A sparkle twinkled in her eye as she pursed her lips together.

Lexy stared out the front window of the bakery, watching the water rush over the falls. She was dying to know what they were up to and had tried to get the information out of Jack the night before but he'd been extremely tight-lipped.

"Can I take a piece back for Ida?" Helen asked.

"Of course! Why don't I box the whole cake up for you guys? I certainly don't need the extra calories here." Lexy jumped up to grab a bakery box from behind the counter.

"It's too bad Ida had to miss seeing it whole," Nans said. "But Norman is in terrible pain. They were talking about giving him oxycontin or morphine to make it more bearable."

"That's pretty strong stuff," Cassie said.

"Jack said something about oxycontin last night in relation to the case he is working. I guess it's one of the prescription drugs that this drug ring specializes in. He's not sure where they get it from." Lexy turned to Nans. "Is that the case you two were working on?"

"Nope." Nans shook her head.

Lexy rolled her eyes and sighed. "You're not going to tell me, are you?"

"You'll find out in good time, dear." Nans reached over and patted her hand.

Before Lexy could press the issue further, Nans's cell phone blared from her purse.

"Hello?" She yelled into the phone, causing Lexy and Cassie to jump. The phone was turned up loud and they could all hear Ida on the other end.

"Mona!" Ida gasped, calling Nans by her given name, "Norman's gout is getting worse. His knees have swollen up like soccer balls. They're going to move him to the nursing care section. He can't walk or even move out of bed ... not even to go to the bathroom."

"Oh dear, that sounds awful."

"I need you guys to come back right away. When they move him over, we're going to have to stand guard twenty-four-seven so that he doesn't become the next victim."

"Don't you worry, we're on it." Nans snapped the phone shut, then looked at the other women around the table.

"Well, you heard her ... let's get a move on."

Lexy eyed the remains of Cassie's practice wedding cake sitting in the middle of Nans's dining room table.

"Help yourself, dear."

Lexy looked down at her stomach. Her pants were just starting to fit normally and she didn't want to risk gaining weight back, even though she was so hungry she felt like passing out. "Thanks, but I'm all set."

Lexy took a seat furthest from the cake and watched Nans pace the room. According to Nans's early morning phone call, she had some "big news" but she wouldn't spill the beans until Ruth and Helen were there.

Finally, a knock sounded at the door and Nans rushed over to let the two women in.

"So, what's so important that you have to call us all here at this hour of the morning?" Ruth hustled into the apartment, a steaming coffee mug already in her hand.

"You won't believe what happened last night!" Nans's face was flushed with excitement, her sharp green eyes twinkled.

Lexy, Ruth and Helen raised their eyebrows.

"What?"

"I was taking my shift, watching Norman last night and at approximately 3:12 AM, I heard some moaning and what sounded like a struggle from the room next door. I turned my hearing aid way up, so I could hear better and I thought I heard someone say *No*. Then I heard a crash." She paused, and Ruth gasped. Lexy leaned forward on the edge of her chair.

"Go on." Helen said, motioning with her hands.

"I ran out into the hallway, and just as I reached the door, who do you think was coming out of that room?"

"Nurse Rothschild!"

"No. The janitor," Nans said. "And he was acting sneaky too. When he saw me, he got all nervous and practically ran down the hall.

Lexy sucked in a breath. "Do you think he tried to kill the person?"

"I don't know. Maybe," Nans said. "I went into the room to make sure the patient was okay. He was, but he looked like he was in pain, thrashing around and stuff. The sliding tray had crashed down onto the floor."

"What did you do?"

"Thankfully a nurse came in and gave him some morphine and picked up the mess."

"Nurse Rothschild?"

"No, I don't think she was on duty last night. At least I didn't see her."

Ruth tapped her finger on her top lip. "So ... maybe we've been wasting our time with the investigation of Rothschild."

Nans nodded. "We'd better start looking into that janitor."

"I still wish we could get a handle on the motive," Helen said.

"And what about the earring I found?" Lexy asked.

Nans walked over to her computer table, pulled the earring out of a drawer and held it up. The gold setting glimmered in the light, a perfect contrast to the black pearl. "It's a very distinctive setting, and very feminine. I doubt the janitor would have been wearing it."

"Maybe it fell off earlier and has nothing to do with the murder," Helen said.

"Or maybe the janitor has an accomplice who wears earrings," Ruth added.

Nans pursed her lips. "We'll have to keep all avenues open. What I heard last night doesn't necessarily mean the janitor is the killer. But it does mean we need to look at him a little closer. I'm not ruling Rothschild out just yet either and, if we can tie the earring to her, all the better."

Nans's iPad started ringing on the table in front of her and she tilted her head to look at the display. "It's Ida calling on Facetime, she's down with Norman," she said, sliding the bar to answer.

Ida's face filled the screen and Lexy felt an icy chill race up her spine at her words.

"Mona, get down here right away. There's been another murder ... and this one doesn't look so natural."

Chapter Thirteen

"It's that room over there." Ida pointed to a room down the hall where there was a bustle of activity. Nans, Ruth and Helen took off toward it with Lexy following slowly behind.

Nans stopped at the doorway. "We can't get in," she whispered. "Helen, see if you can get some pictures with your camera glasses."

Lexy followed Helen, standing on her tippy toes and craning her neck to look into the room. Inside, a body lay at an odd angle on the bed. The pillows were tossed on the floor and the sheets were bunched up. Some members of the staff stood around, their faces masks of concern.

Lexy caught the eye of Cassie's cousin Sam, who flitted nervously at the end of the bed. She raised her eyebrows and jerked her head to get Sam to come out into the hallway.

"What's going on?" Lexy asked.

Sam took a deep breath. "It looks like Mr. Turco has been killed." She glanced back into the room. "We're waiting for the police."

Lexy felt her heart lurch. Would Jack be coming here? She didn't know if it was such a good idea for him to find her here given the current tension between them on the subject of her investigating murders.

"Why would someone kill him?" Lexy asked.

Sam started to chew her bottom lip. "No one knows. He was in a lot of pain, maybe someone wanted to put him out of his misery."

"Do you have any idea who that might be?"

Sam glanced up the hallway, moved a step closer to Lexy and lowered her voice. "I've been thinking about how you asked about Nurse Rothschild the other day and you're right. She isn't a kind and caring nurse. I think it could have been her."

Lexy felt her heartbeat speed up. "Do you have any proof?"

"No ... just a feeling."

"Move it along, ladies." One of the nurses came out into the hall, giving Sam a pointed look, then shooing Lexy, Nans, Ruth, and Helen down the hall away from the room. Ida popped her head out of a room at the end of the hallway and beckoned them inside.

"Did you see anything?" Ida asked in a hushed tone.

"Too many people in there," Nans replied. "How's Norman?"

Lexy looked at the bed where Norman lay sleeping. He looked tired and worn.

"He's doing okay. The pain meds really knock him out so I'm just letting him sleep."

Lexy heard a commotion in the hall and felt her stomach drop when she saw Jack accompanied by a crew of police. As if feeling her gaze, he glanced over, his face registering surprise when he recognized her. Lexy gave him a smile and half wave.

"Jack's here," Lexy whispered to the other women.

"Oh good," Nans said. "Is he coming over?"

"Yep." Lexy felt a pit of doom in her stomach. She started to get a little light-headed and nauseous and her annoying eye twitch started up again. Her legs threatened to collapsed out from under her. She folded herself into a chair and put her head between her legs just as Jack strode into the room.

"Lexy ... are you okay?" His voice was peppered with concern.

"Uh-huh. I forgot to eat breakfast this morning and got a little light headed is all," she said from in between her legs.

Jack squeezed the back of her neck. "Are you still dieting? I told you I was only kidding. You look fine. Perfect."

Lexy felt her heart flutter and lifted her head. "Thanks."

"So, you guys finally see that something suspicious is going on here," Nans said.

"Yeah, looks like the killer botched the job. Maybe someone came by before they were done. Anyway, it definitely looks like this one was murder," Jack said looking over at the door. "I can't say about the others though."

"Do you have a suspect?"

"I just got here. Haven't even had a chance to properly look at the scene."

"We have a couple of suspects if you want to know what we've found," Nans offered.

Jack narrowed his eyes at her. "How did you girls get down here so fast, anyway?"

"My boyfriend, Norman, is here with the gout and I happened to be visiting and heard the commotion." Ida nodded toward Norman, still asleep in the bed.

Jack raised an eyebrow at Nans, Ruth and Helen.

"Ida called us and we came right away," Nans said.

"And you, Lexy?" Lexy felt her stomach flutter as Jack directed his gaze toward her.

"I just happened to be visiting Nans." She shrugged.

"Okay, well I have to get to work, but I want you ladies to be very careful. I have a hunch about this case and, if I'm right, we could be dealing with someone desperately dangerous." Jack's face was grim as he looked at each of them. "I don't want any of you to get hurt."

He bent down and kissed Lexy's forehead. "And that goes double for you," he said, then strode out of the room.

Chapter Fourteen

Lexy's stomach groaned, her mouth watered as Nans set the spinach omelet in front of her.

"Eat this dear, it will give you some energy."

She dug into the egg before Nans even finished the sentence. She ate ravenously, stopping only long enough to jab at her eye which was still twitching.

Helen sat across from her, watching her eat. "You know I can stop that twitching with some simple hypnosis."

"Yeah, I've been thinking about that ... it *is* pretty annoying, but I'm not sure I believe in hypnosis."

"Nonsense. I hypnotized you before, remember?"

It was true. When Lexy had stumbled across the body of a client, Helen had hypnotized her to remember the details of the crime scene. It had been easy and painless.

"Well, it would be nice to get rid of the twitch." Lexy narrowed her eyes at Helen. "No funny stuff, though."

"Of course not, I never do anything like that, right girls." Helen looked back at Nans and Ruth, who were listening while putting the pictures from the camera glasses up on the computer.

Nans and Ruth mumbled in agreement, then the pictures flashed on the screen and captured everyone's attention.

Lexy polished off the omelet, put her dish in the sink and joined them over at the computer. The pictures didn't reveal much. The body, the disarray of the bedding and a few personal items on the bedside table.

"I don't see any clues in there," Lexy said.

"Me either," Nans replied. "Anyone else see anything?"

Ruth and Helen shook their heads.

"Maybe once we have time to think about it, something will stand out," Nans made her way over to the coffee machine and poured coffee for everyone.

Lexy took hers gratefully, the mug warming her hands. She breathed in the welcoming, bittersweet aroma of the coffee and took a sip.

"Ahhh...," she said, poking at her eye.

"Okay, now to take care of that eye twitch." Ruth pulled a chair up beside her, took her hand and started to murmur soothing words. Lexy felt relaxed and almost laughed thinking that her eyelids really were getting heavy.

The next thing she knew, she was putting down her cup of coffee amidst laughter from the three women on the other side of the table.

Lexy felt her cheeks grow warm. "What are you laughing at?"

"Oh nothing dear. You shouldn't be bothered by that eye twitch ever again," Ruth said, patting her knee.

"Thanks." Lexy rubbed at her eye. It *had* stopped twitching, which was good, but what was up with all the laughing?

Nans turned to look at the pictures on the computer screen. "Now that the police believe us, maybe we'll be able to solve this faster."

"Lexy, I assume you'll be seeing Jack tonight?" Ruth raised an eyebrow at her.

"I'm not sure, maybe."

"You should make it a point to. Find out what he knows about the investigation so far. That will really help us. And, of course, you can share the clues we have found with him too," Nans said.

Lexy bit the inside of her cheek. She'd have to tread very carefully with Jack, but she felt a renewed determination to get him to give in and let her investigate these murders.

"Maybe I'll make his favorite dessert at the bakery today and surprise him with it tonight."

"The way to a man's heart is through his stomach ... maybe it's also the way to get him to give up clues and information," Ruth said, causing them all to laugh.

Lexy felt a renewed vigor and energy, which made her a little suspicious when she remembered how Alma at Sunny Acres had a renewed sense of energy after Helen had hypnotized her. She wondered what else Helen might have done during her hypnosis session.

She glanced over at the other woman with narrowed eyes. Helen looked back with an innocent smile. Lexy did a mental head-shake. Of course Helen hadn't hypnotized in any "extras", that was ridiculous. The energy was probably from the eggs, after all she hadn't been eating well lately so it was no wonder a good meal would make her feel invigorated.

She glanced at her watch and felt a zing of adrenalin. "I better get going, Cassie is expecting me at the bakery."

"Okay, dear. Can you come here tomorrow before you go to the bakery and fill us in on what you heard from Jack? I'll fix you a nice breakfast." Nans knew the bribe of a hot meal was just the thing to get Lexy out of bed early.

"You've got yourself a deal." Lexy said, then drained the last of her coffee.

Cluck!

"Did you hear that?" Lexy asked.

"Hear what?" Nans replied.

"I didn't hear anything," Ruth offered.

"Me either," Helen said.

"I thought I heard a duck or some bird." Lexy narrowed her eyes at the three women. Three sets of innocent eyes stared back at her.

"Must have been outside," Nans said.

Lexy shrugged and put her coffee mug in the sink. Grabbing her jacket from the coat rack beside the door, she bid the women good-bye. As she shut the door, she could have sworn she heard the three ladies laughing on the other side.

Chapter Fifteen

Lexy slipped the form-fitting black cashmere sweater over her head and turned sideways to inspect herself in the mirror. It looked perfect with her faded jeans. She had to admit, she looked pretty good—casual but sexy, and the best part was the outfit was comfortable.

Now all she had to do was sweeten Jack up with dinner, dessert, and wine, and he'd be primed to spill all his secrets about the case.

She raced down the stairs, two at a time and into the kitchen. The salmon was marinating in a lime and honey concoction, and potatoes were baking in the oven. Sprinkles sat in front of her bowl, expectantly.

"You want to eat now?"

Sprinkles answered by doing a little dance, her toenails clicking on the tile floor. Lexy fed the dog, then set about cutting up some broccoli for the steamer. Her stomach rumbled, reminding her that she hadn't eaten since Nans had cooked her the omelet that morning. She felt a little weak and dizzy, but had opted to save all her calories for the meal she was preparing to share with Jack.

She dumped the broccoli into the steamer, pulled the potatoes from the oven and set the salmon under the broiler just in time to hear Jack's tap at the window of her kitchen door.

"Well, hello gorgeous." Lexy felt her cheeks grow warm as Jack's gaze raked her body when she opened the door for him. He put the wine he'd brought down on the counter and pulled her to him.

Lexy melted into him as his lips claimed hers. She felt dizzy from his kiss ... or maybe it was from the lack of food. Either way, the kiss was a good sign that Jack wasn't mad at her for being at the crime scene.

The buzzer on the stove interrupted them, and she pulled away to check the salmon. Lexy noticed that Jack's hands were a little unsteady as he poured two glasses of wine.

"This smells delicious," he said leaning over the salmon and inhaling deeply. She saw his eyes cut to the glass topped pie stand on the counter. "Is that a coconut cream pie?"

Lexy beamed. "Yes, I made it for you today at the bakery." Coconut cream was his favorite—if anything could get him to open up about the investigation, it was a coconut cream pie.

Lexy deftly cut the salmon, buttered the potatoes, and divided the broccoli between two plates, then set them on the table. Jack pulled out Lexy's chair and they sat opposite each other to eat.

Lexy felt light-headed as she sipped her wine. She wondered if she should have eaten before starting in on the wine, but the alcohol gave her the extra courage she needed to start the conversation about the investigation.

"So, did you find out anything about the murder at the retirement center?" she ventured.

"What?" Jack looked up at her with a blank stare, making it clear his thoughts were off somewhere else.

"I was asking about the murder at the retirement center ... did you find any clues?"

"Oh." Jack wrinkled his brow. "Not really. We're looking into the usual suspects--family and people at the retirement center, but we don't have anything concrete."

"Do you think there's anything in common with the other people who died?"

"We haven't looked into the other people because we don't know for sure that they were murdered."

Lexy stabbed a spear of broccoli with her fork and raised an eyebrow at him. "But if they were ..."

"If they were, the only thing they have in common that I know of is that they were in the nursing care section."

Lexy sighed and nibbled off a teensy piece of the broccoli. "Maybe the reason they were in nursing care is what they have in common."

Jack pushed his salmon around. "You might not be too far off. I have a gut feeling that the deaths have something to do with the drug ring investigation I'm in the middle of."

Lexy's eyes went wide. "You think the drugs might be coming from the retirement center?"

Jack shrugged. "Maybe." He went back to pushing his food around on his plate. Lexy realized that he hadn't eaten much. Her stomach felt hollow, and not just from the lack of food ... something seemed off with Jack.

"Is everything okay?" she asked.

Jack's fork clattered onto the plate and and he fumbled with picking it up again. Was that sweat on his brow? Lexy's heart seized with dread—something *was* wrong.

"Lexy, I have something to say."

A wave of dizziness swept over her at the serious look on his face. Was he breaking up with her? Because she kept getting involved in these investigations? Her mind went back to the kiss they had shared when he first came in. *Surely he wouldn't kiss her like that if he was going to dump her?*

The room started to swim before her eyes with the combination of nervousness and lack of food. Jack must have dropped something on the floor because she saw him get down on his knees to retrieve it. Lexy looked down at the floor to see what it was and the next thing she knew the floor was rushing up to meet her in the face.

Then everything went black.

###

Lexy opened her eyes to see Sprinkles looking down at her from an impossible angle. How could the dog be above her? The only way that could happen was if she were laying down, which judging by the hard floor pressed against her back, she probably was.

"Lexy, are you okay?" She heard Jack's voice.

She took a mental inventory of her body. "Yes, I think so. What happened?" She asked, bringing her arms up to fend off the barrage of kisses that Sprinkles bathed her face with.

"I think you passed out. Did you eat anything today?"

"I had an omelet this morning."

"Jesus, Lexy, that's not enough." Jack pulled her up from the floor, brushed off her backside, then put his hands on her upper arms, bending his tall frame to stare into her eyes. "You have to start eating more. You're not fat. In fact, I think you're just perfect."

Lexy's heart jerked in her chest as he bent down and brushed his lips against her forehead, then gently maneuvered her into her chair.

"Now eat." He pointed to her plate, then went over and started the coffee machine on the counter.

Lexy dug into the salmon and potato. She had to admit, she *was* starving. Jack replaced her wine glass with a coffee mug and sat down on his side of the table watching her eat in silence. She couldn't help the little "nummy" sounds that came out of her mouth.

She finished up and pushed her plate away feeling encouraged that Jack had also devoured most of his meal. The food was doing it's job, she felt a lot stronger and not so dizzy. She took a sip of coffee and closed her eyes.

"Did you just cluck?"

"What?" Lexy furrowed her brow. Did he say *cluck*?

"I thought I heard you make a strange noise." Jack shrugged, then grabbed both of their plates and dumped them in the sink.

Lexy stood up to liberate the pie from its glass display. Her heart skipped a beat, remembering how Jack had been acting before she passed out. *What was he up to?*

"It seemed like you were going to say something important before I passed out." She handed him a plate loaded with a thick, tall slice of pie.

Jack smiled and put the pie on the counter, pulling her into his arms instead.

"I was, but it can wait until you're feeling one hundred percent better." He traced the tip of his finger down the side of her neck causing her body to shiver with anticipated pleasure. "Right now, I think we have some other important business to tend to."

Chapter Sixteen

"Would you guys like to test out another one of my new recipes?" Lexy opened the cardboard bakery box, and produced a tray of aromatic white chocolate biscotti which she placed in the center of Nans's dining room table.

"More biscotti?" Ruth asked as she, Helen and Nans picked a biscuit from the plate. Lexy had already helped herself and bit into the confection, the white chocolate dip coated her tongue with a creamy sweetness, which was the perfect compliment to the dark blend coffee that was sending up spirals of steam on the table in front of her.

She took a sip.

Nans, Helen and Ruth laughed. Lexy louvered her eyes at them. "What's so funny?"

"Nothing," Helen said, her eyes wide. "Did the hypnosis work for your eye tic?"

Lexy realized that her eye hadn't bothered her the previous night when she'd been nervous about Jack's behavior. "Well, it hasn't bothered me, but I think I need more time to know for sure."

"Oh, I'm sure it worked." Helen said, amidst more laughter from the other women.

Ruth finished off her biscotti, adjusted her dentures and brushed the crumbs off her shirt. "That was delicious—I'd say you have a winner on your hands."

Lexy felt a swell of pride when the other women nodded their agreement.

"Now, let's get down to business." Nans put her elbows on the table and leaned across toward Lexy. "What did Jack have to say about the case?"

"Not much, I'm afraid. He's still not convinced the first two were murdered." Lexy's stomach dropped at the disappointed looks on the women's faces. "But he did say he had a suspicion the murder might be tied to the drug ring case he is working on."

"Really?" Helen asked. "How so?"

"Apparently the drug ring sells quite a bit of oxycontin. They don't know where it is coming from. You need a prescription for it, so it has to be tied to some place medical. He was starting to think it might be coming from the retirement center because the hospitals and doctors' offices have such strict rules."

"I don't see how they would actually get the drugs to sell them, I mean I'm sure they are carefully watched here too. But that *is* something we should look into," Ruth said.

"I researched the janitor, Sam Turner. He has some financial problems. That would be motivation for stealing drugs and selling them on the black market. Janitors don't make very much money, you know," Helen said.

"That's very interesting," Nans nibbled on the end of her second biscotti. "I happened to talk to the person who was staying in the room with Bertram Glumm when he was murdered. I asked

137

him who was in there and he didn't remember seeing Nurse Rothschild, but he did say he remembered Sam being there."

Helen and Ruth gasped.

"Wait a minute," Helen said." Who was Bertram's roomie?"

"Willard Stevens," Nans winced.

"Oh, he's practically senile!" Ruth said.

"That explains why he didn't notice a murder happening right in the next bed." Lexy rolled her eyes.

"Well, he *is* hard of hearing and maybe a little forgetful, but he did say he remembered that night. He said the curtain was drawn around the bed all night which he thought was odd. At least it's something to think about."

"Looks like all fingers point to the janitor, Sam," Ruth said. "And that's good because I found out that nurse Rothschild couldn't have committed the last murder. She wasn't working at the time."

Lexy's eyebrows rose a few notches. "Interesting. So that rules her out? She could still be in on it with Sam … or maybe she snuck back in to do the murder."

"True. But I think we can put her on the back burner and turn up the heat on Sam," Nans said. "But I still don't understand how the murders would tie in to stealing drugs. I'm not convinced they are related."

A couple of taps sounded on the door and they all turned toward it in time to see Ida bustle in, leading with her left hand, on which sat a new sparkling diamond ring.

"Guess what, girls!"

They all stood and leaned over her hand.

"It's gorgeous!"

"Gigantic."

"He proposed in the nursing care ward?"

Ida giggled like a schoolgirl. "Yes, I guess he was planning on doing it and didn't want to wait just because he was laid up."

Lexy felt her heart squeeze. Was everyone *except* her getting engaged? She immediately regretted her jealous thoughts. She was happy for Cassie and Ida, heck, she didn't even know if she *wanted* to get married. Her and Jack didn't always see eye to eye, so maybe it would be a mistake. Still, it would be nice to be asked.

They all got in line to hug and congratulate Ida. Lexy pulled Ida's hand up to her face to admire the ring. It was very similar to Cassie's.

Crap!

She'd forgotten that Cassie's dress rehearsal was tonight. She glanced at her watch, her stomach clenching. She had forty-five minutes to get home, change and then over to the restaurant where Cassie planned to get married. She pushed away from the group.

"I gotta run, I'm late for Cassie's wedding rehearsal!" She said, grabbing her coat and bolting out the door.

Chapter Seventeen

Lexy rushed into the entrance of the Brook Ridge Falls restaurant. Her hair sat piled on top of her head in an unruly mess, her dress needed adjustment and she sported sneakers on her feet instead of the Manolo Blahnik rhinestone-studded stilettos she planned to wear for the wedding. But at least she'd made it on time ... almost.

The restaurant, an old mill, boasted a gigantic picture window with a spectacular up-close view of the waterfall. Cassie, John, and Jack stood in a huddle in front of it.

Jack turned as she approached, his face blanched and he shoved something into his pocket. Her eyes narrowed as she saw him say something to the others and they whirled around to look at her. *Why was everyone acting so strange?*

Her disturbing thoughts fled and her eyes widened as she got the full view of Cassie in her deep red gown, hair highlighted to match. She had accentuated the outfit with black rhinestone jewelry and a black veil which hung from the back of her head. *Stunning.*

"You look amazing!" she said, making Cassie blush.

"You look pretty good yourself," Jack said, his eyes traveling down her body and back up to her eyes. Lexy's heart flip-flopped in her chest as a smile lit his handsome face.

"Oh, well, I kind of got ready in a hurry." She shrugged, reaching up to straighten her messy hair.

"Yeah, you usually have much better shoe choices," Cassie said, causing Lexy's cheeks to grow warm as everyone looked down at her sneakers.

Thankfully, the minister interrupted their inspection of her footwear. "Are we ready to start?"

Cassie looked around the room. "I think everyone is here, so I guess so. We're having a lattice archway made with red roses that we'll stand under." She walked over to the center of the window. "I'd like to put it here. We'll stand facing the waterfall and you can stand here facing us."

Cassie pointed to a spot and the minister obediently stood there. Cassie and John took their places in front of him.

"Wait," Cassie said. "I need a stand in so I can see how this looks." She grabbed Lexy and put her in the bride's spot, then shoved John out of the way and replaced him with Jack. "Stay there so I can see how it will look from the guests' point of view."

Lexy glanced at Jack out of the corner of her eye. He looked impossibly handsome in his tux. When he turned to look at her, she felt a little weak in the knees. Until she noticed how nervous he looked. *Was standing at the altar with her that nerve wracking?*

"That's perfect." Cassie's voice pulled her from her thoughts and she turned in time to see her friend walking back to take her place, a devious gleam in her eye. "How did it feel for you two to be standing in front of the minister?" She cocked an eyebrow at Jack who shuffled backwards, his hands held up in the air.

"I wouldn't want to steal the limelight from you and John," he said, pushing John back into the groom's spot.

The minister cut in. "Will someone be walking you down the aisle?"

"My brother," Cassie motioned for her brother, Brandon, to join them.

"Wow, you look dapper." Lexy admired Brandon. He owned a fitness studio and his muscular body was evident under the tux.

"You too," he said, then glanced down at her shoes. "Almost."

Lexy swatted at him playfully. Cassie and Brandon were close and, since Lexy and Cassie had been best friends for decades, Brandon was like a brother to her.

The minister ushered them all to the back of the room and they were joined by Cassie's cousins, Sam and Justine, and another cousin Mick. The minister paired off the wedding party and they practiced marching down the aisle.

Lexy couldn't help but feel all warm and fuzzy when she saw the look on John's face as he stood at the altar waiting for Cassie to join him. She hoped someday she would have someone waiting up there for her with the same look on his face. *Would that* somebody *be Jack?*

Eventually they got it perfect and retired to the bar to celebrate. Lexy ordered a coffee. She sauntered over toward Sam, who sat with her elbows propped on the bar, her hand curled around a bottle of beer. Now was the perfect time to try to get more information about the murders out of her.

"Hi," Lexy cupped her hands around the coffee mug to warm them. The restaurant was chilly inside and the sleeveless dress didn't provide much in the way of warmth.

"Hey Lexy, have you heard any more about what happened at the retirement center yesterday?" Sam asked.

"Not too much, what about you?"

"Isn't that the police detective who was there?" Sam tilted the top of her beer bottle towards Jack.

"Yes, he works with John."

"Oh, thats right. Sometimes I forget that Cassie is marrying a cop." Sam swiveled her chair to face Lexy. "She never used to like them. But if the rest of them are as good looking as those two, I can see the attraction."

Lexy leaned against the bar, ignoring the pang of jealousy she felt when she saw the way Sam looked at Jack.

"I was wondering, what happens after someone dies at the retirement center?" Sam's perplexed look invited her to elaborate. "Specifically, what's the procedure. I mean, do you call the police for all of them ... or the funeral home?"

"Well the last one, Mr. Turco, was clearly not natural so, of course we called the police for that. But the others, if the doctor on duty deems the death to be of natural causes we just call the next of kin and the funeral home. It's usually listed in their files."

"What happens to their belongings?"

Sam pursed her lips. "Why? Are you thinking that's why they were killed?"

"Maybe."

"Their clothing and other effects go to the family."

Lexy chewed her bottom lip, trying to think up the right way to phrase her next question.

"What about their medications?"

Sam's eyes grew wide, her hand jerked, spilling her beer on the bar.

"Crap!" She jumped away from the bar looking down at the stain on her dress. She glanced up at Lexy, her eyes darting wildly, then ran off in the direction of the ladies room. Lexy grabbed a pile of napkins and mopped up the spill.

A bit of an over-reaction to a beer spill. Lexy stared after Sam, then finished the clean up and took a sip of her coffee.

"Did you say something?"

Jack appeared at her elbow, startling her out of her thoughts. She narrowed her eyes at him.

"No." *Had* she said something out loud?

"Oh, it sounded like you made a clucking sound."

"What?"

"You know, like a chicken."

Lexy furrowed her brow. This wasn't the first time she'd been accused of clucking recently and it was starting to get as annoying as the eye tic. Something in the corner of her mind nagged at her, but she was distracted by Sam coming back into the room.

She noticed Jack looking at Sam too, and felt a bit envious of how Sam's figure filled her dress out perfectly. Lexy looked down at her own figure and wondered if she still needed to lose a few pounds from her hips.

She looked back at Sam. The other woman looked more put-together in her outfit. A nice pair of heels, glittery earrings, and a necklace that complimented the dress perfectly.

Lexy leaned forward, squinting her eyes to see the necklace better, her heart freezing in her chest. The gold chain glittered with reflection from the chandeliers overhead, but that wasn't what caught her attention. It was the pendant in the center. A black pearl in a unique setting.

Lexy realized Jack had been chatting away beside her. She clutched at his arm to get him to stop, and whipped her head around to face him.

"I think I know who the killer is."

Lexy pulled Jack aside into the corner of the room and watched his face as she told him her suspicions about the killer.

"That makes sense, but I need some evidence," Jack said, running his hand through his hair.

"But if we don't do something fast, someone else might get killed." Lexy's thoughts turned to Norman who lay in the nursing care center. If her suspicions were correct, he fit the killer's profile perfectly, and she feared he may be next.

"I know, Lexy, but my hands are tied."

Lexy chewed her bottom lip. "What if we caught the killer in the act?"

"That would be pretty hard to do considering we don't know when they will strike next. We don't have the man power to stake out the retirement center indefinitely."

Lexy glanced at him out of the corner of her eye. "We could make it irresistible for the killer, then we'd know exactly when they were going to strike and we could be there to catch them in the act."

He raised an eyebrow at her. "You mean a setup?"

Lexy nodded. "Would that be dangerous?"

Jack rubbed his chin with his thumb. "Not necessarily. We've done that sort of thing before. It's all carefully monitored so the decoy is never really in any danger." He narrowed his eyes at Lexy. "Did you have someone in particular in mind?"

Lexy's stomach lurched. She *did* have someone in mind, but she didn't want to put anyone in danger.

"Yes, but we'll have to see if she agrees, and you'll have to swear she won't get hurt."

Jack put his hand on Lexy's arm. "Of course I would never put anyone in danger, especially the person you have in mind," he said, with a wink. "Now, let's get out of here so I can put the plan into action.

Chapter Eighteen

Nans lay in the small hospital bed, her heart pounding so hard that it seemed like everyone in the retirement center could hear it. She wiped her sweaty palms on the sheets, and tried to feign sleep.

Despite her high level of anxiety, the background noise in the critical care center lulled her senses. She'd lain there for hours and was starting to feel sleepy, despite her fears. Struggling to stay awake, she congratulated herself on being wily enough to tuck the sleeping pill the nurse's aid had given her under her tongue so she could spit it out after she left.

She wasn't sure if she'd drifted off, but her body was relaxed on the bed when she heard someone tip-toe softly into the room. Immediately, she went into high alert, every nerve tingling while she tried to remain perfectly still under the sheets.

"Mona?" The voice was just above a whisper.

She didn't move or answer. She heard the sound of soft-soled shoes creeping closer to the bed.

"Are you awake?" The voice was right next to her ear and it was all Nans could do not to jump at the sound.

Nans's heart jerked in her chest as she felt a pillow slide out from under her head, then felt it slowly pressed over her face—lightly at first, then with increasing pressure until she couldn't suck in any more air.

Her mind whirled in panic. Someone was supposed to be here to help her!

She couldn't stop her body from struggling as it tried in vain to pull in oxygen. The edges of her consciousness started to go gray. She felt her stomach drop as she started to submit to the darkness. *Something had gone terribly wrong.*

"Hold it right there!"

Nans's heart leaped with relief as she heard Jack's voice loud and clear. The pressure on the pillow eased up and she sucked in a lungful of air.

Lexy rushed to her side, and grabbed her hand. She looked up in time to see Jack shoot her a look of concern as he took out his handcuffs.

"Nans, are you all right?" Lexy cried.

Sucking in another breath, she found her voice.

"Of course, I'm all right. No thanks to you people. What the *hell* took you so long."

Epilogue

Lexy took her almond biscotti and dunked it in her coffee. Nibbling off a corner, she glanced around the front room of her bakery where they had pulled two of the cafe tables together in order to accommodate the large group celebrating the arrest of the retirement center killer.

To her left, Cassie and Ida were comparing their engagement rings. Lexy tried not to feel envious. She was happy for them, even if her relationship with Jack wasn't quite working out the way she wanted.

Her eyes darted around the group and came to rest on Jack who was seated as far from her as possible. Her heart faltered when their eyes met and he looked away from her quickly. He'd been acting stranger than strange lately and she found it too stressful. She was going to have to come right out and ask him what was going on.

"I still don't understand how the murders enabled Sam to get oxycontin to sell on the black market." Lexy heard Ruth say to Jack.

"Anyone in the nursing care facility who was on pain killers had the prescriptions filled ahead of time. The pills were doled out as needed by the nurses but when someone died, all their pills were disposed of. Once prescribed, you can't reuse them so the staff would flush them." Jack said. "Instead of Sam flushing them, she pocketed them and sold them later on."

"That explains why the people were killed shortly after they were admitted. There would be more drugs in the hopper," Nans said.

Lexy glanced over at Cassie, whose cheeks were red enough to match her hair. "I feel so bad about this ... I didn't have any idea what she was up to."

Nans reached over and patted her hand. "Of course you didn't dear, it's not your fault."

"It wasn't just Sam," Jack added, "The leaders of the ring would get people in their debt and then try to place them at nursing homes and force them to get the drugs. Thanks to your information, we were able to break up the whole ring, so hopefully our senior citizens will be safe now."

Lexy thought of the suspicious deaths at Sunny Acres and felt a cold chill, wondering how many other people had died in other nursing homes.

"Lexy, how did you put it all together?" Helen asked, helping herself to a lemon biscotti from one of the plates which were piled full of different flavors of the crunchy concoction.

"Just a lucky break. I happened to notice the necklace she had on at Cassie's rehearsal matched the earring we found under the bed. Then I remembered she'd acted kind of strange when I saw her dispensing drugs at the retirement home, and when I asked what happened to the medication when people died, she got all nervous." Lexy shrugged. "Then when I remembered that Cassie said she used to be into drugs, it all kind of came together."

"Now I realize when Bertram Glumm's roommate said he saw "Sam" in the room, he was talking about Cassie's cousin, not Sam, the janitor!" Nans said.

Lexy took a sip of her coffee. She closed her eyes and welcomed the bitter brew, then opened them quickly when she realized everyone was laughing at her.

"What is going on?"

Nans looked at Helen. "Should we tell her?"

Helen nodded. "Remember when I hypnotized you?"

Lexy narrowed her eyes, looking from Helen to Ruth to Nans to Ida. "Yeeees."

"Well, I did sort of give you something extra." The four ladies giggled.

"But don't worry," Ruth said. "It will wear off as time goes on."

Lexy remembered back to the hypnosis session at Sunny Acres and how Helen had given Alma a renewed zest and energy.

"Is it a renewed sense of energy?" Lexy asked.

"Not exactly." Helen scrunched her face up.

"It's got something to do with why people seem to keep laughing at me, doesn't it?"

Nans nodded. "We had a little fun with you, dear, and Helen implanted a suggestion that you cluck like a chicken sometimes when you take a sip of coffee."

The four older women burst out laughing and were soon joined by everyone at the table—everyone, except Lexy.

"What?" Lexy felt her face growing warm.

"Sorry, dear. We don't get to have too much fun like that. It will happen less and less as time goes on." Helen said in between snickers.

Lexy felt her mouth drop open. "So, you've all been laughing at me behind my back?"

"Oh come on now, Lexy, the ladies were just having a little fun. No harm was done, right?" Jack said, spreading his arms.

Lexy stared at him. Another time she might have laughed it off, but now, looking at Jack, she felt her anger rising.

"Well, that's easy for you to say. I think you owe me some explanations too," she said.

A hush fell on the table.

"Huh?"

"You've been acting all secretive. Doing weird things, like not letting me go in your living room, sneaking off with Nans, and whispering with everyone here," she spread her hands to indicate the people at the table. "If there's something going on, I think I deserve to know."

She stood up, slamming her palm on the table while everyone stared at her open-mouthed.

Jack rubbed his face with his hands. He looked worn and tired making Lexy immediately regret her outburst. He stood up. "There *is* something we need to talk about, but not here." He crossed over to her, took her by the elbow and dragged her outside.

Lexy's heart-beat drummed in her ears as he turned her to face him. *Had she been too hasty?* His six foot frame seemed to tower over her and she bit back tears.

She glanced back into the bakery and noticed everyone looking out at them, their eyes wide, faces practically pressed to the glass. She felt the sting of humiliation flame her cheeks. *Was everyone going to watch Jack break up with her?*

She looked back at him, her stomach sinking as she watched him take a deep breath.

"Lexy, there has been something I've been meaning to say. But ... well ... It's never been the right time, or I've chickened out."

She felt frozen in the spot, unable to speak. Jack shuffled his feet, barely able to look her in the eye.

Well, if he's going to dump me, he might as well just get on with it, she thought. She straightened her back and crossed her arms in front of her, waiting for the break-up speech.

Jack tried to take her hand, but she pulled it away.

He reached into his pocket, took something out and then bent down on one knee.

Lexy's heart skipped wildly in her chest as she stared at the tiny, black velvet box he held in his hand.

He looked up at her, his face mixed with fear and hope.

"Lexy, will you marry me?"

The End.

Recipes

Black Bean Brownies

This recipe comes from a book I publish under another pen name which is a compilation of my favorite recipes adapted to use healthy ingredients. The book is Healing Desserts by Lee Anne Dobbins (you can get it for your kindle too!)

I first heard about the recipe at a Pampered Chef party and came up with my own version below.   At first I couldn't believe that brownies made from beans could taste good, but they do! They are also healthy for you - the beans add a ton of healthy antioxidants and nutrients as well as fiber. I use agave nectar instead of sugar because it is healthier but if you can't find agave, you can just use the same amount of sugar.

Ingredients:

1 (15.5 ounce) can black beans, rinsed and drained
1/4 cup cocoa powder (with over 70% cocoa if you can find it)
3 eggs
3 tablespoons vegetable oil (or coconut oil for a healthier alternative)
3/4 cup agave nectar (or sugar if you don't have agave)
1 pinch salt
1 teaspoon vanilla extract
1 teaspoon instant coffee
1/2 cup milk chocolate chips (optional)

Preparation:

Preheat oven to 350F.

Combine beans, cocoa, eggs, oil, agave (or sugar), salt, vanilla and coffee in a food processor and process until smooth.

Pour mixture into a greased 8 x 8 pan.

Sprinkle chocolate chips over the top (if desired).

Bake for 30 minutes until the edges start to pull away from the pan.

###

Lemon Biscotti

I love the hard crunchy texture of biscotti. This recipe could be adapted for a variety of flavors - you can use orange zest instead of lemon zest, or leave the zest out all together and use different flavored extract like almond or anise.

Ingredients:

1 cup white sugar
1/2 cup vegetable oil
3 eggs
1 tablespoon vanilla extract
2 tablespoons grated lemon zest
3 1/4 cups flour
1 tablespoon baking powder

Preparation:

Preheat the oven to 375F.

Beat the sugar, oil, eggs and vanilla extract together in a large bowl.

Add the lemon zest to the egg mixture and mix well.

In a smaller bowl, sift the flour and baking powder together.

Add the flour mixture to the egg mixture.

Let the dough sit for 5 minutes.

Divide the dough into two balls. Roll the balls to be the length of a cookie sheet.

Put the rolls on the cookie sheet and press down to about 1/2" thick.

Bake for 25 minutes until golden brown. Let them cool for about 5 minutes, then slice them into 1" slices. Put the slices cut side up on the cookie sheet and cook for another 10 – 15 minutes until golden brown.

For added pizzaz, you can melt chocolate and dip one end of each cookie in the chocolate after they have cooled completely.

A Note From The Author

Thanks so much for reading my cozy mystery "*3 Bodies and a Biscotti*". I hope you liked reading it as much as I liked writing it. If you did, and feel inclined to leave a review over at Amazon, I really would appreciate it.

This is book four of the Lexy Baker series, you can find the rest of the books on my website, or over at Amazon if you want to read more of Lexy's and Nans's adventures.

Also, if you like contemporary humorous romance, you might like my book "*Reluctant Romance*" which has lots of romance, suspense, conflict and even a couple of dogs. I have an excerpt from it at the end of this book.

This book has been through many edits with several people and even some software programs, but since nothing is infallible (even the software programs) you might catch a spelling error or mistake and, if you do, I sure would appreciate it if you let me know - you can contact me at lee@leighanndobbs.com.

Oh, and I love to connect with my readers so please do visit me on facebook at http://www.facebook.com/leighanndobbsbooks or at my website http://www.leighanndobbs.com.

Are you signed up to get notifications of my latest releases and special contests? Go to: http://www.leighanndobbs.com/newsletter and enter your email address to signup - I promise never to share it and I only send emails every couple of weeks so I won't fill up your inbox.

About The Author

Leighann Dobbs lives in New Hampshire with her husband, their trusty Chihuahua mix Mojo and beautiful rescue cat, Kitty. She likes to write romance and cozy mystery novelettes perfect for the busy person on the go. These stories are great for someone who doesn't have a lot of time for reading a full novel. Why not pick one up and escape to another time and place the next time you are waiting for an appointment, enjoying a bath or waiting to pick up the kids at soccer?

Find out about her latest books and how to get her next book for free by signing up at:

http://www.leighanndobbs.com

Connect with Leighann on Facebook and Twitter

http://facebook.com/leighanndobbsbooks

http://twitter.com/leighanndobbs

More Books By This Author:

Blackmoore Sisters
Cozy Mystery Series
* * *

Dead Wrong

Lexy Baker
Cozy Mystery Series
* * *

Killer Cupcakes
Dying For Danish
Murder, Money and Marzipan
Brownies, Bodies and Bad Guys

Contemporary
Romance
* * *

Sweet Escapes
Reluctant Romance

Dobbs "Fancytales"
Regency Romance Fairytales Series
* * *

Something In Red
Snow White and the Seven Rogues

###

Excerpt From Backmoore Sisters Cozy Mystery Series Book 1 (Dead Wrong):

Morgan Blackmoore tapped her finger lightly on the counter, her mind barely registering the low buzz of voices behind her in the crowded coffee shop as she mentally prioritized the tasks that awaited her back at her own store.

"Here you go, one yerba mate tea and a vanilla latte." Felicity rang up the purchase, as Morgan dug in the front pocket of her faded denim jeans for some cash which she traded for the two paper cups.

Inhaling the spicy aroma of the tea, she turned to leave, her long, silky black hair swinging behind her. Elbowing her way through the crowd, she headed toward the door. At this time of morning, the coffee shop was filled with locals and Morgan knew almost all of them well enough to exchange a quick greeting or nod.

Suddenly a short, stout figure appeared, blocking her path. Morgan let out a sharp breath, recognizing the figure as Prudence Littlefield.

Prudence had a long running feud with the Blackmoore's which dated back to some sort of run-in she'd had with Morgan's grandmother when they were young girls. As a result, Prudence loved to harass and berate the Blackmoore girls in public. Morgan's eyes darted around the room, looking for an escape route.

"Just who do you think you are?" Prudence demanded, her hands fisted on her hips, legs spaced shoulder width apart. Morgan noticed she was wearing her usual knee high rubber boots and an orange sun-flower scarf.

Morgan's brow furrowed over her ice blue eyes as she stared at the older woman's prune like face.

"Excuse me?"

"Don't you play dumb with me Morgan Blackmoore, what kind of concoction did you give my Ed? He's been acting plumb crazy."

Morgan thought back over the previous weeks customers. Ed Littlefield *had* come into her herbal remedies shop, but she'd be damned if she'd announce to the whole town what he was after.

She narrowed her eyes at Prudence. "That's between me and Ed."

Prudence's cheeks turned crimson. Her nostrils flared. "You know what *I* think," she said narrowing her eyes and leaning in towards

Morgan, "I think you're a witch, just like your great-great-great-grandmother!"

Morgan felt an angry heat course through her veins. There was nothing she hated more than being called a witch. She was a Doctor of Pharmacology with a Master Herbalist's license, not some sort of spell-casting conjurer.

The coffee shop had grown silent. Morgan could feel the crowd staring at her. She leaned forward, looking wrinkled old Prudence Littlefield straight in the eye.

"Well now, I think we know that's not true," she said, her voice barely above a whisper. "Because if I was a witch, I'd have turned you into a newt long ago."

Then she pushed her way past the old crone and fled out the coffee shop door.

***

Fiona Blackmoore stared at the amethyst crystal in front of her wondering how to work it into a pendant. On most days, she could easily figure out exactly how to cut and position the stone, but right now her brain was in a pre-caffeine fog.

Where was Morgan with her latte?

She sighed, looking at her watch. It was ten past eight, Morgan should be here by now, she thought impatiently.

Fiona looked around the small shop, *Sticks and Stones*, that she shared with her sister. An old cottage that had been in the family for generations, it sat at one of the highest points in their town of Noquitt, Maine.

Turning in her chair, she looked out the back window. In between the tree trunks that made up a small patch of woods, she had a bird's eye view of the sparkling, sapphire blue Atlantic ocean in the distance.

The cottage sat about 500 feet inland at the top of a high cliff that plunged into the Atlantic. If the woods were cleared, like the developers wanted, the view would be even better. But Fiona would have none of that, no matter how much the developers offered them, or how much they needed the money, her and her sisters would never sell the cottage.

She turned away from the window and surveyed the inside of the shop. One side was setup as an apothecary of sorts. Antique slotted shelves loaded with various herbs lined the walls. Dried weeds hung from the rafters and several mortar and pestles stood on the counter, ready for whatever herbal concoctions her sister was hired to make.

On her side, sat a variety of gemologist tools and a large assortment of   crystals. Three antique oak and glass jewelry cases displayed her creations. Fiona smiled as she looked at them. Since childhood she had been fascinated with rocks and gems so it was no surprise to anyone when she grew up to become a gemologist and jewelry designer, creating jewelry, not only for it's beauty, but also for it's healing properties.

The two sisters vocations suited each other perfectly and they often worked together providing customers with crystal and herbal healing for whatever ailed them.

The jangling of the bell over the door brought her attention to the front of the shop. She breathed a sigh of relief when Morgan burst through the door, her cheeks flushed, holding two steaming paper cups.

"What's the matter?" Fiona held her hand out, accepting the drink gratefully. Peeling back the plastic tab, she inhaled the sweet vanilla scent of the latte.

"I just had a run in with Prudence Littlefield!" Morgans eyes flashed with anger.

"Oh? I saw her walking down Shore road this morning wearing that god-awful orange sunflower scarf. What was the run-in about this time?" Fiona took the first sip of her latte, closing her eyes and waiting for the caffeine to power her blood stream. She'd had her own run-ins with Pru Littlefield and had learned to take them in stride.

"She was upset about an herbal mix I made for Ed. She called me a witch!"

"What did you make for him?"

"Just some Ginkgo, Ginseng and Horny Goat Weed... although the latter he said was for Prudence."

Fiona's eyes grow wide. "Aren't those herbs for impotence?"

Morgan shrugged "Well, that's what he wanted."

"No wonder Prudence was mad...although you'd think just being married to her would have caused the impotence."

Morgan burst out laughing. "No kidding. I had to question his sanity when he asked me for it. I thought maybe he had a girlfriend on the side."

Fiona shook her head trying to clear the unwanted images of Ed and Prudence Littlefield together.

"Well, I wouldn't let it ruin my day. You know how *she* is."

Morgan put her tea on the counter, then turned to her apothecary shelf and picked several herbs out of the slots. "I know, but she always seems to know how to push my buttons. Especially when she calls me a witch."

Fiona grimaced. "Right, well I wish we *were* witches, then we could just conjure up some money and not be scrambling to pay the taxes on this shop and the house."

Morgan sat in a tall chair behind the counter and proceeded to measure dried herbs into a mortar.

"I know. I saw Eli Stark in town yesterday and he was pestering me about selling the shop again."

"What did you tell him?"

"I told him we'd sell over our dead bodies." Morgan picked up a pestle and started grinding away at the herbs.

Fiona smiled. Eli Stark had been after them for almost a year to sell the small piece of land their shop sat on. He had visions of buying it, along with some adjacent lots, including, interestingly enough, that of Pru and Ed Littlefield in order to develop the area into high end condos.

Even though their parents early deaths had left Fiona, Morgan and their two other sisters property rich, but cash poor the four of them agreed they would never sell. Both the small shop and the stately ocean home they lived in had been in the family for generations and they didn't want *their* generation to be the one that lost them.

The only problem was that, although they owned the properties outright, the taxes were astronomical and, on their meager earnings, they were all just scraping by to make ends meet.

All the more reason to get this necklace finished so I can get paid. Thankfully, the caffeine had finally cleared the cobwebs in her head and Fiona was ready to get to work. Staring down at the amethyst, a vision of the perfect shape to cut the stone appeared in her mind. She grabbed her tools and started shaping the stone.

Fiona and Morgan were both lost in their work. They worked silently, the only sounds in the little shop being the scrape of mortar on pestle and the hum of Fiona's gem grinding tool mixed with a few melodic tweets and chirps that floated in from the open window.

Fiona didn't know how long they were working like that when the bell over the shop door chimed again. She figure it must have been an hour or two judging by the fact that the few sips left in the bottom of her latte cup had grown cold.

She smiled, looking up from her work to greet their potential customer, but the smile froze on her face when she saw who it was.

Sheriff Overton stood in the door flanked by two police officers. A toothpick jutted out of the side of Overton's mouth and judging by the looks on all three of their faces, they weren't there to buy herbs or crystals.

Fiona could almost hear her heart beating in the silence as the men stood there, adjusting their eyes to the light and getting their bearings.

"Can we help you?" Morgan asked, stopping her work to wipe her hands on a towel.

Overton's head swiveled in her direction like a hawk spying a rabbit in a field.

"That's her." He nodded to the two uniformed men who approached Morgan hesitantly. Fiona recognized one of the men as Brody Hunter, whose older brother Morgan had dated all through high school. She saw Brody look questioningly at the Sheriff.

The other man stood a head taller than Brody. Fiona noticed his dark hair and broad shoulders but her assessment of him stopped there when she saw him pulling out a pair of handcuffs.

Her heart lurched at the look of panic on her sister's face as the men advanced toward her.

"Just what is this all about?" She demanded, standing up and taking a step toward the Sheriff.

There was no love loss between the Sheriff and Fiona. They'd had a few run-ins and she thought he was an egotistical bore and probably crooked too. He ignored her question focusing his attention on Morgan. The next words out of his mouth chilled Fiona to the core.

"Morgan Blackmoore...you're under arrest for the murder of Prudence Littlefield."